A Fitz and Cleo Book

Fitz AND Cleo

Jonathan Stutzman & Heather Fox

SQUARE FISH

Henry Holt and Company
New York

D0067589

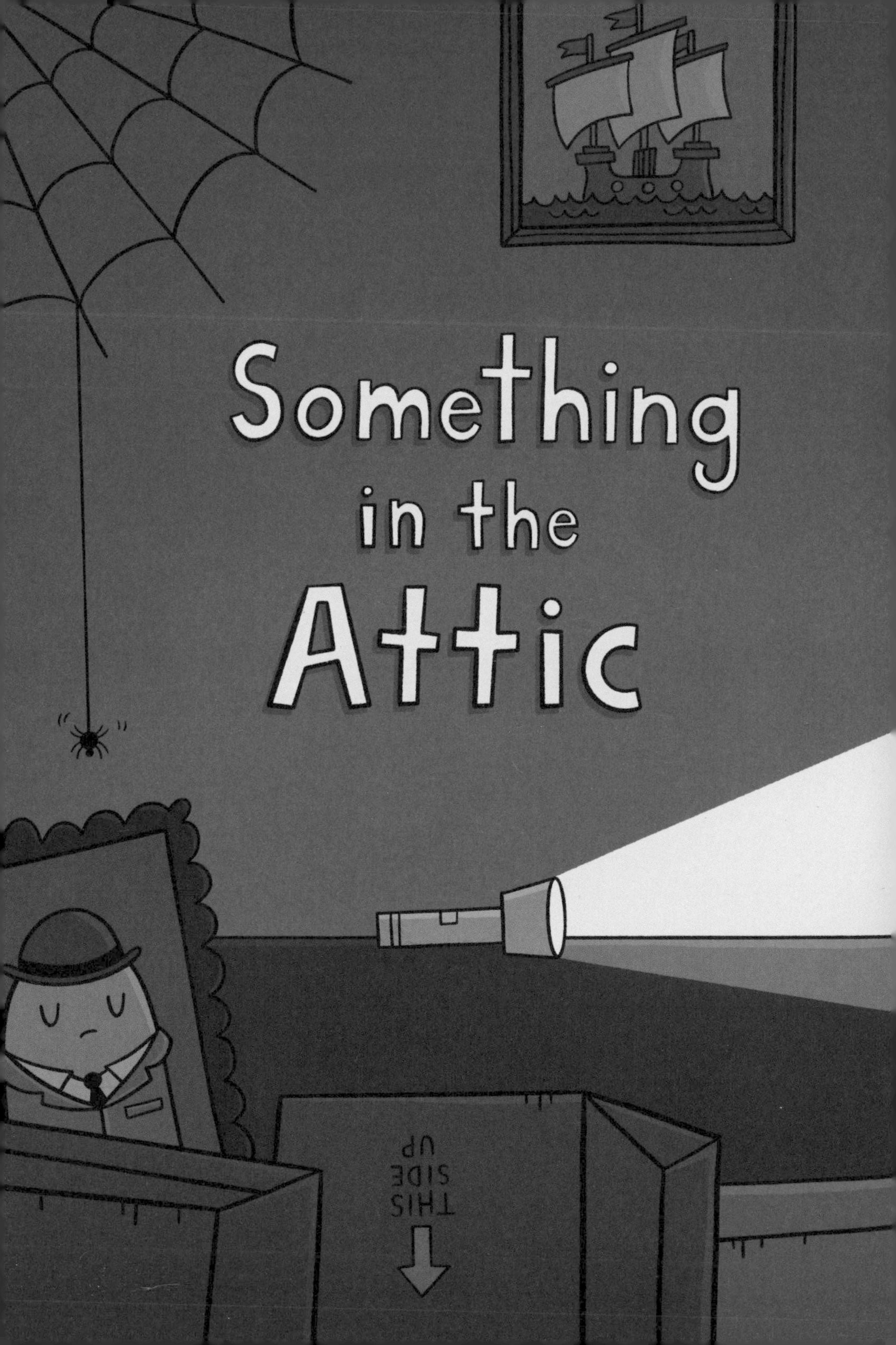
Something in the Attic
THIS SIDE UP

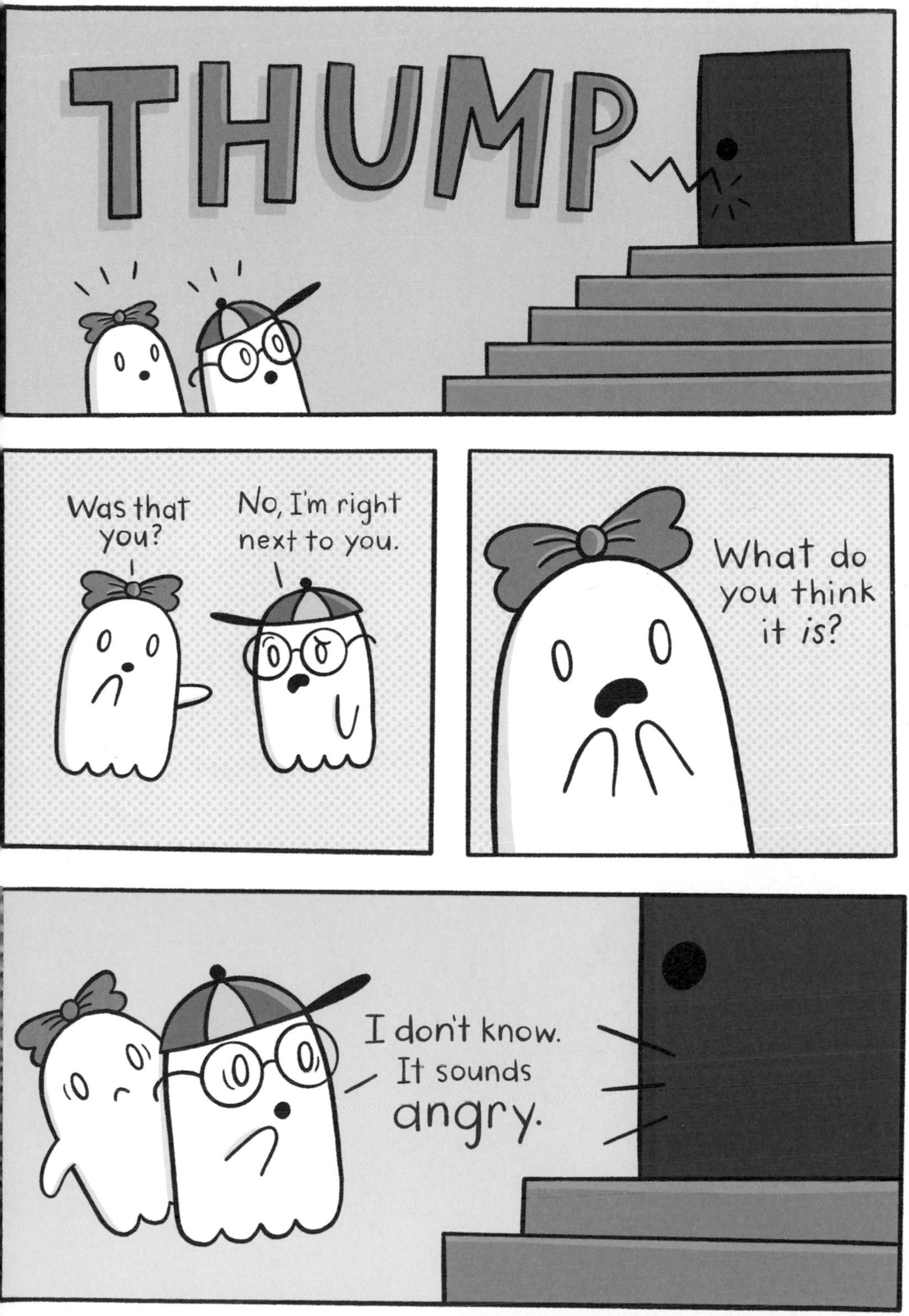
THUMP
Was that you?
No, I'm right next to you.
What do you think it *is*?
I don't know. It sounds angry.

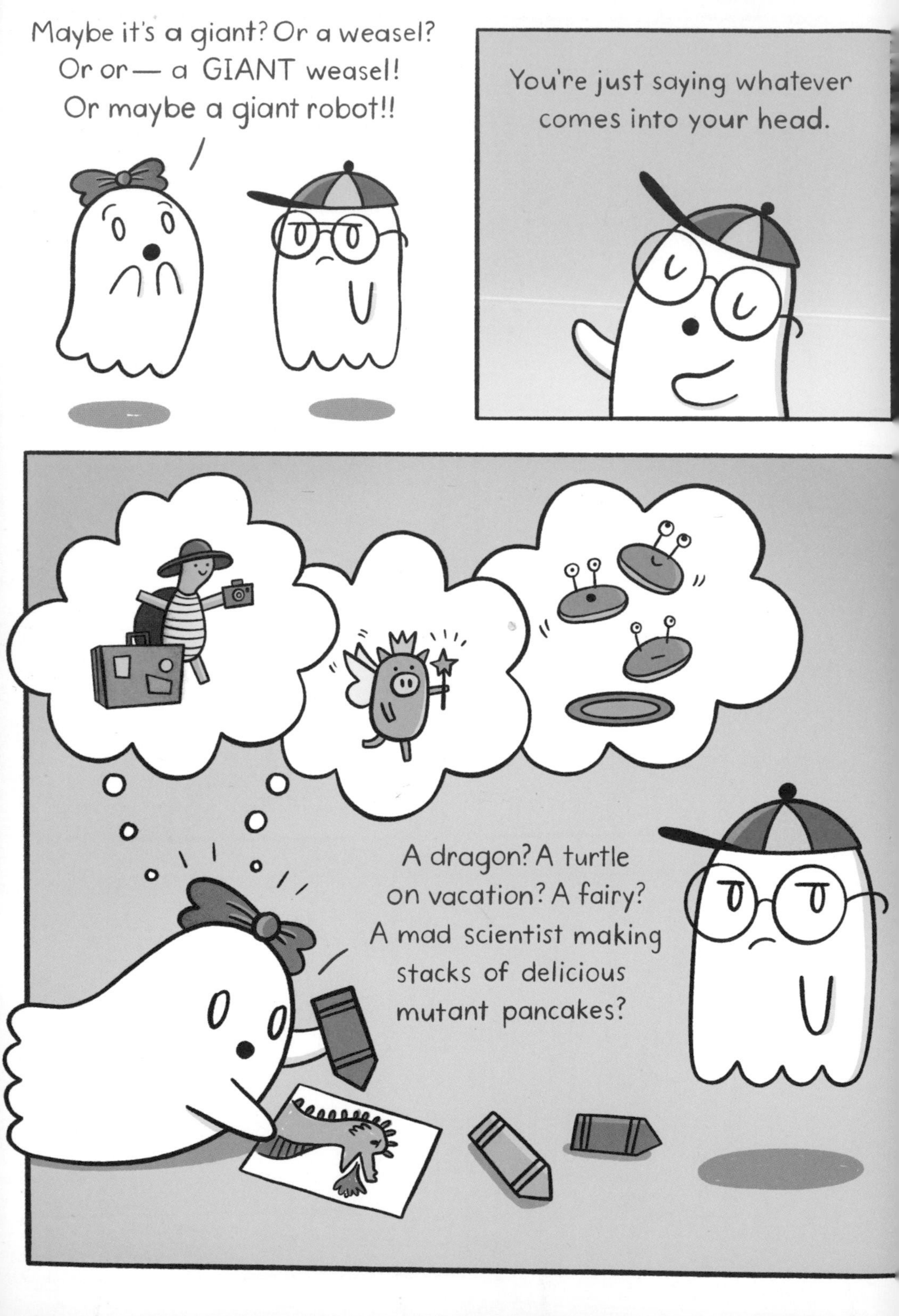
Maybe it's a giant? Or a weasel? Or or— a GIANT weasel! Or maybe a giant robot!!
You're just saying whatever comes into your head.
A dragon? A turtle on vacation? A fairy? A mad scientist making stacks of delicious mutant pancakes?

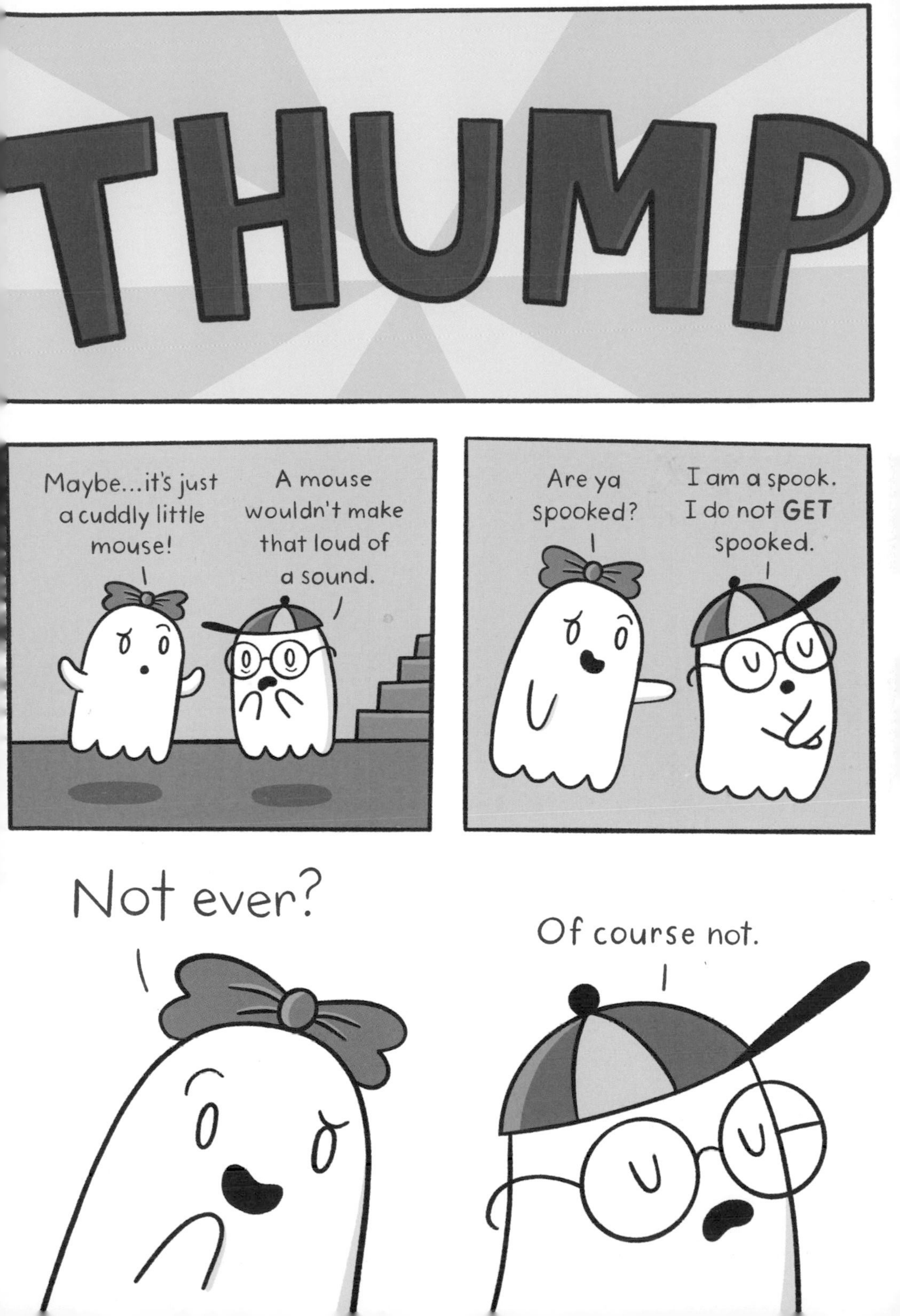
THUMP
Maybe...it's just a cuddly little mouse!
A mouse wouldn't make that loud of a sound.
Are ya spooked?
I am a spook. I do not GET spooked.
Not ever?
Of course not.

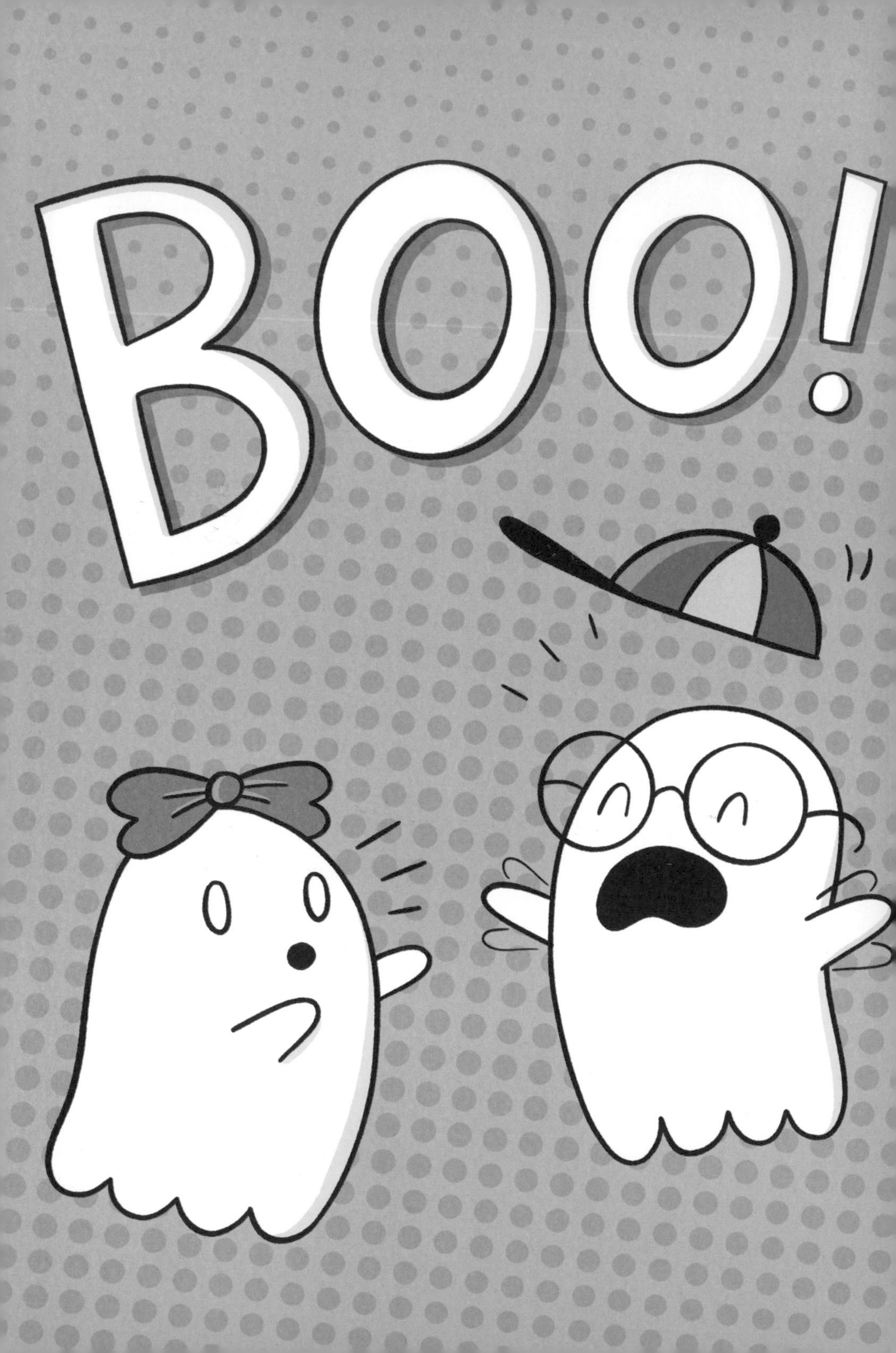
BOO!

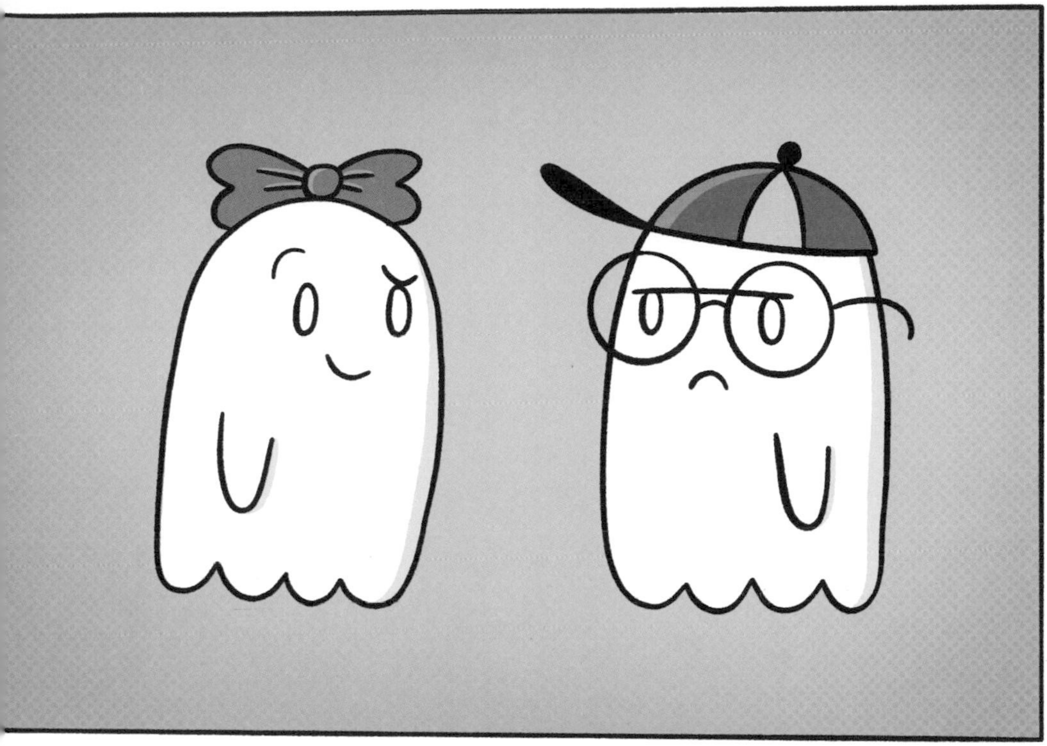

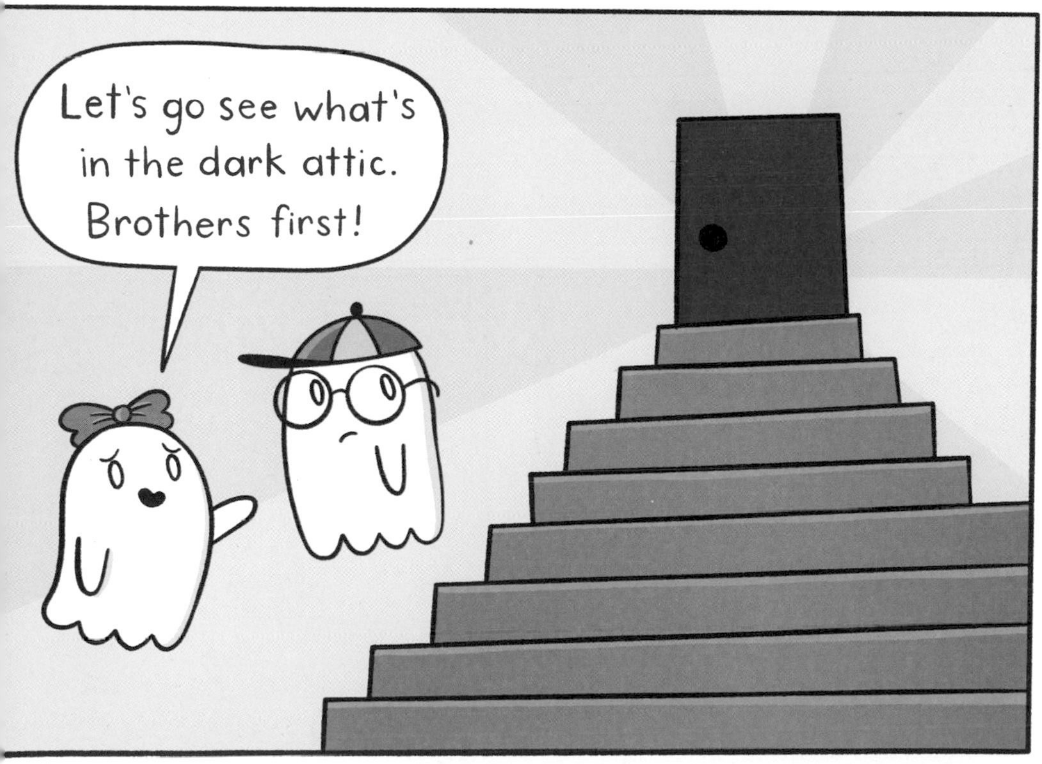
Let's go see what's in the dark attic. Brothers first!

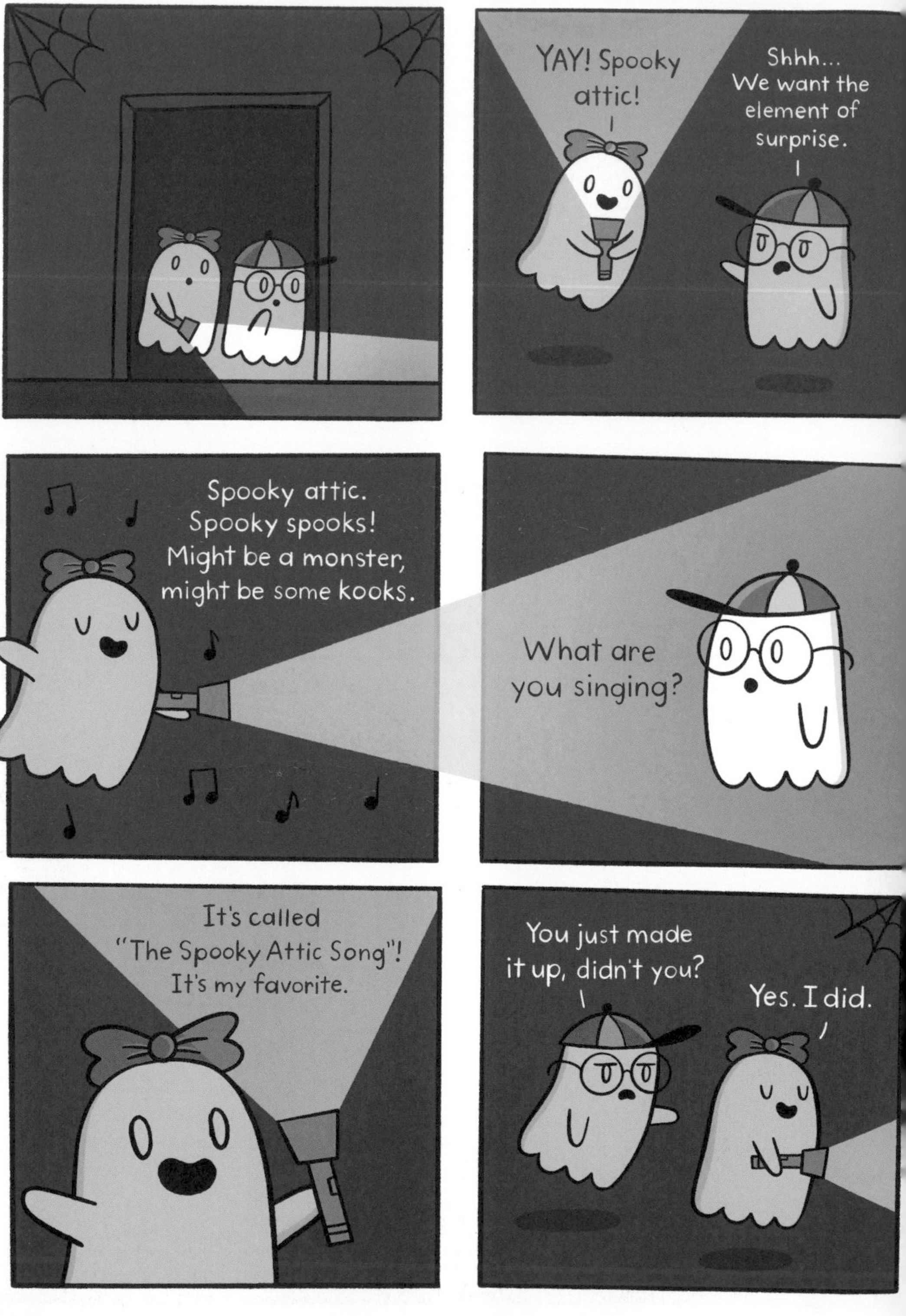
YAY! Spooky attic!
Shhh... We want the element of surprise.
Spooky attic. Spooky spooks! Might be a monster, might be some kooks.
What are you singing?
It's called "The Spooky Attic Song"! It's my favorite.
You just made it up, didn't you?
Yes. I did.

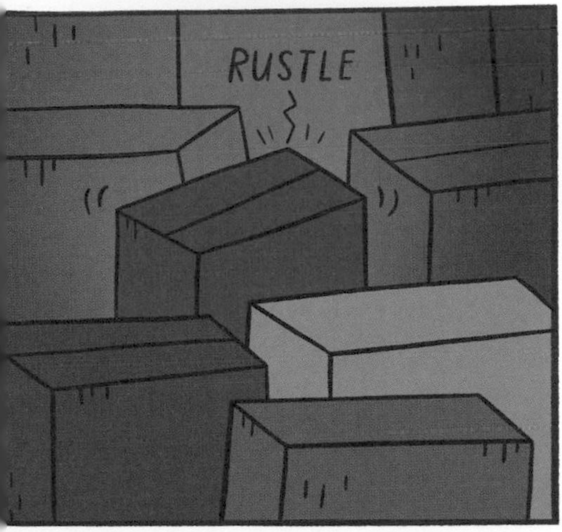
RUSTLE

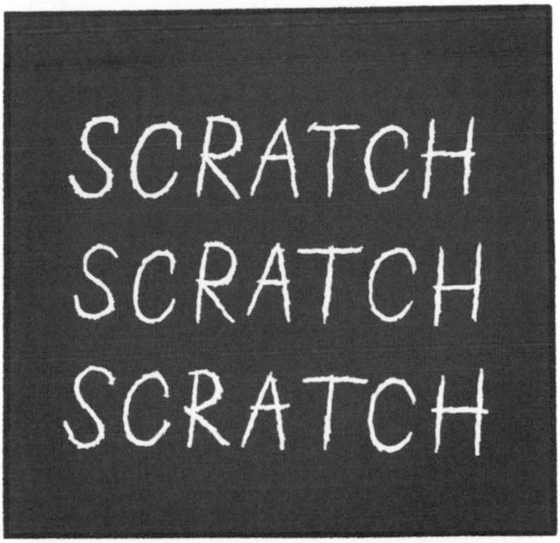
SCRATCH
SCRATCH
SCRATCH

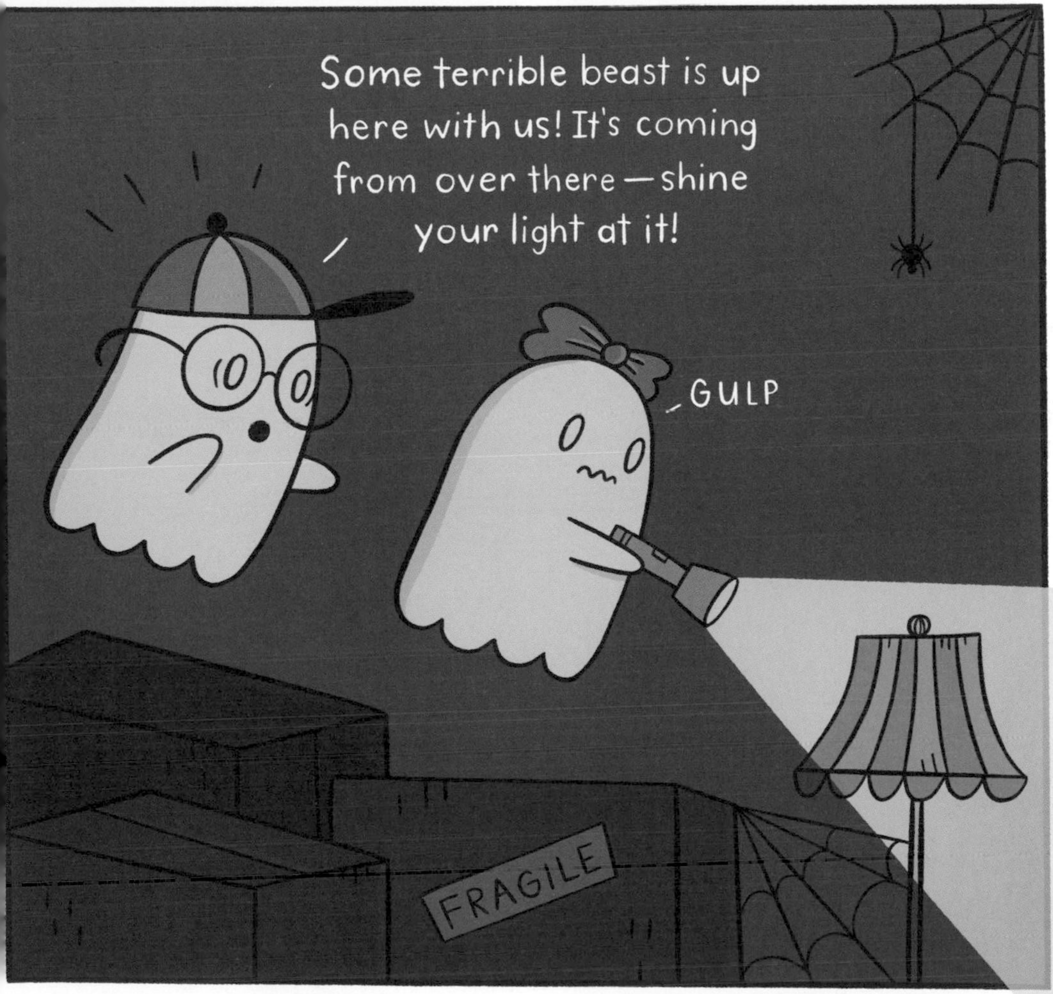
Some terrible beast is up here with us! It's coming from over there—shine your light at it!
GULP
FRAGILE

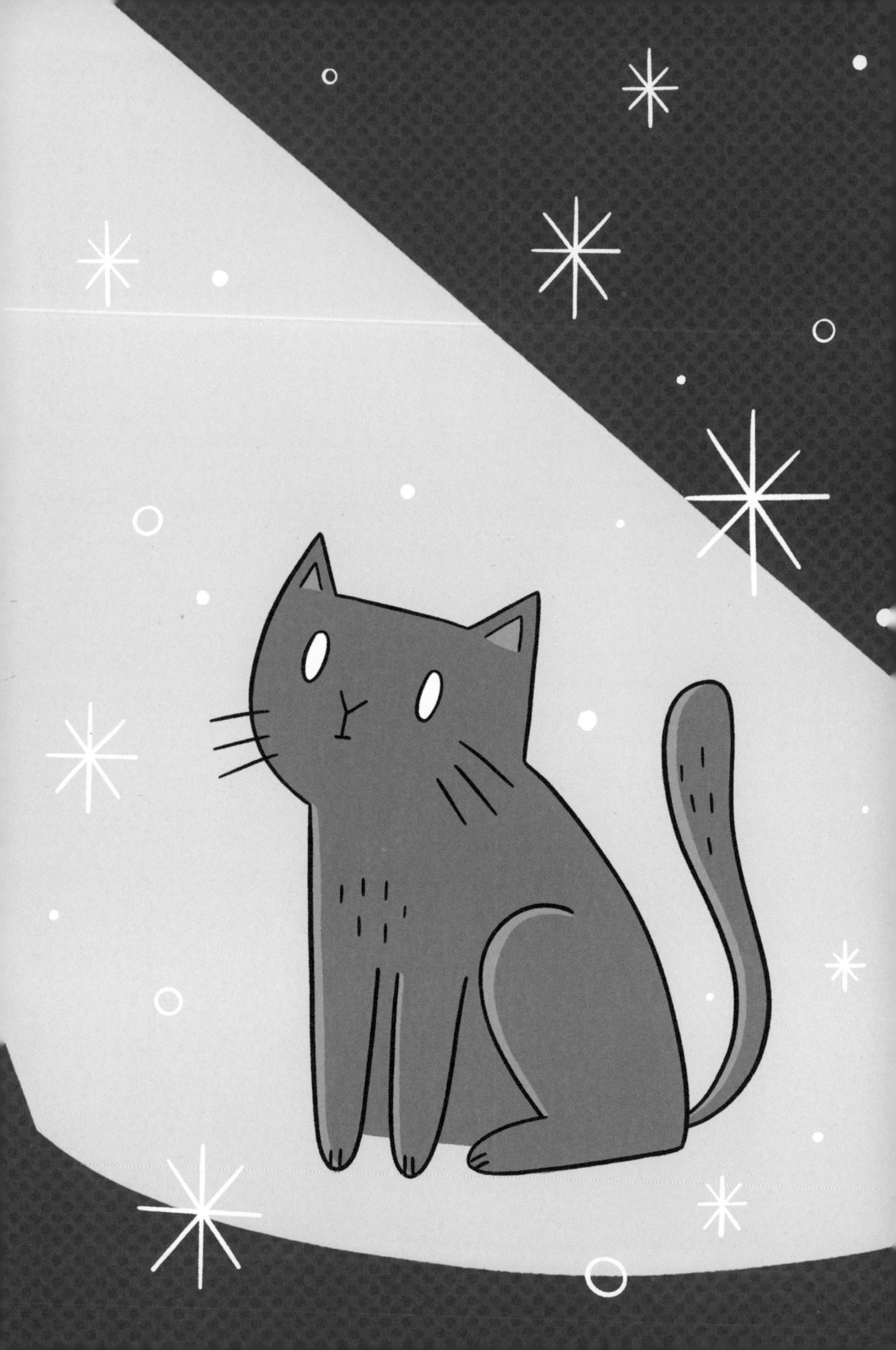

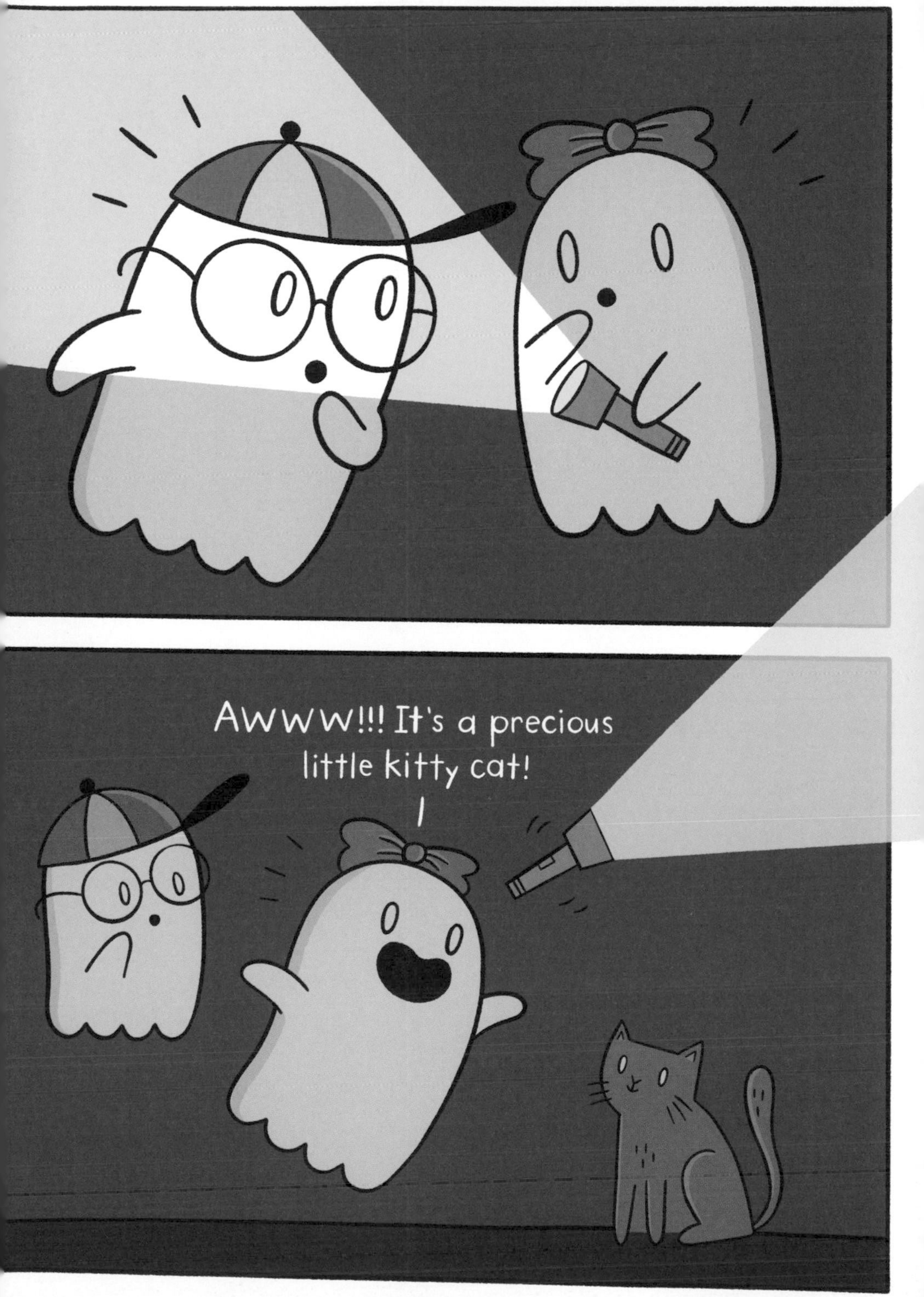
AWWW!!! It's a precious little kitty cat!

I will call him Mister Boo! I love you, Mister Boo! I will love you forever and ever and ever and ever and—

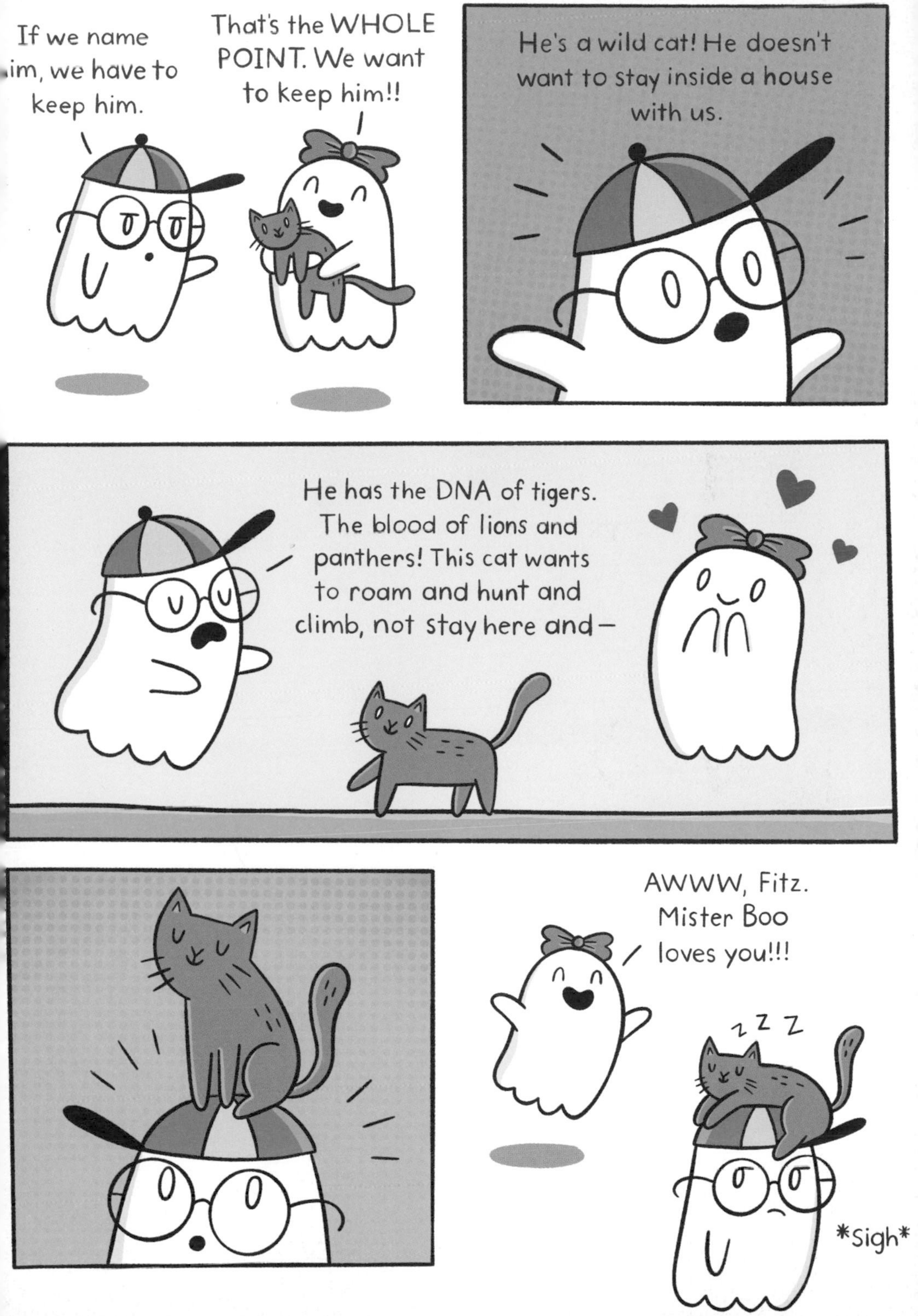

If we name him, we have to keep him.
That's the WHOLE POINT. We want to keep him!!
He's a wild cat! He doesn't want to stay inside a house with us.
He has the DNA of tigers. The blood of lions and panthers! This cat wants to roam and hunt and climb, not stay here and—
AWWW, Fitz. Mister Boo loves you!!!
Z Z Z
Sigh

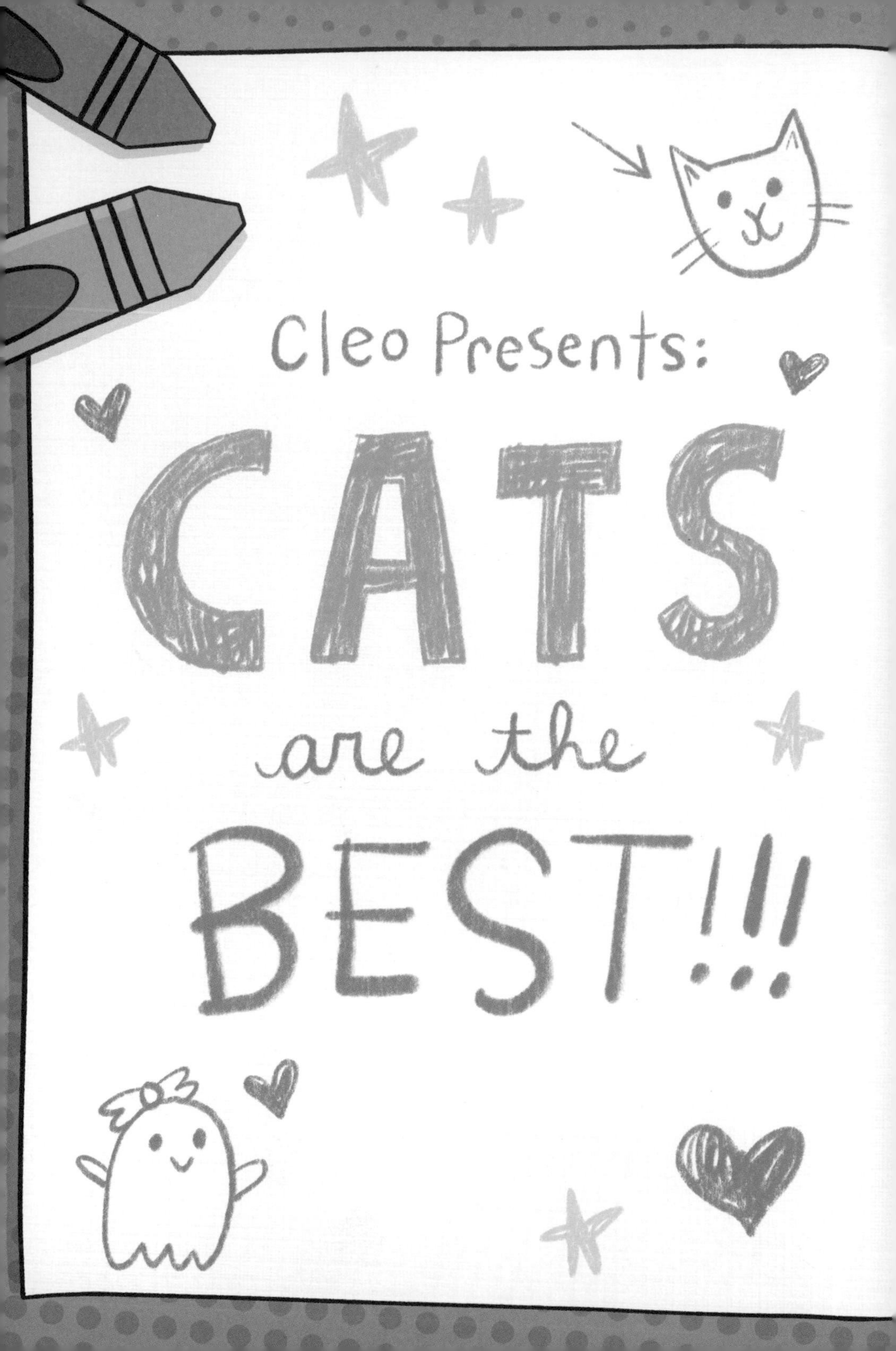
Cleo Presents:
CATS
are the
BEST!!!

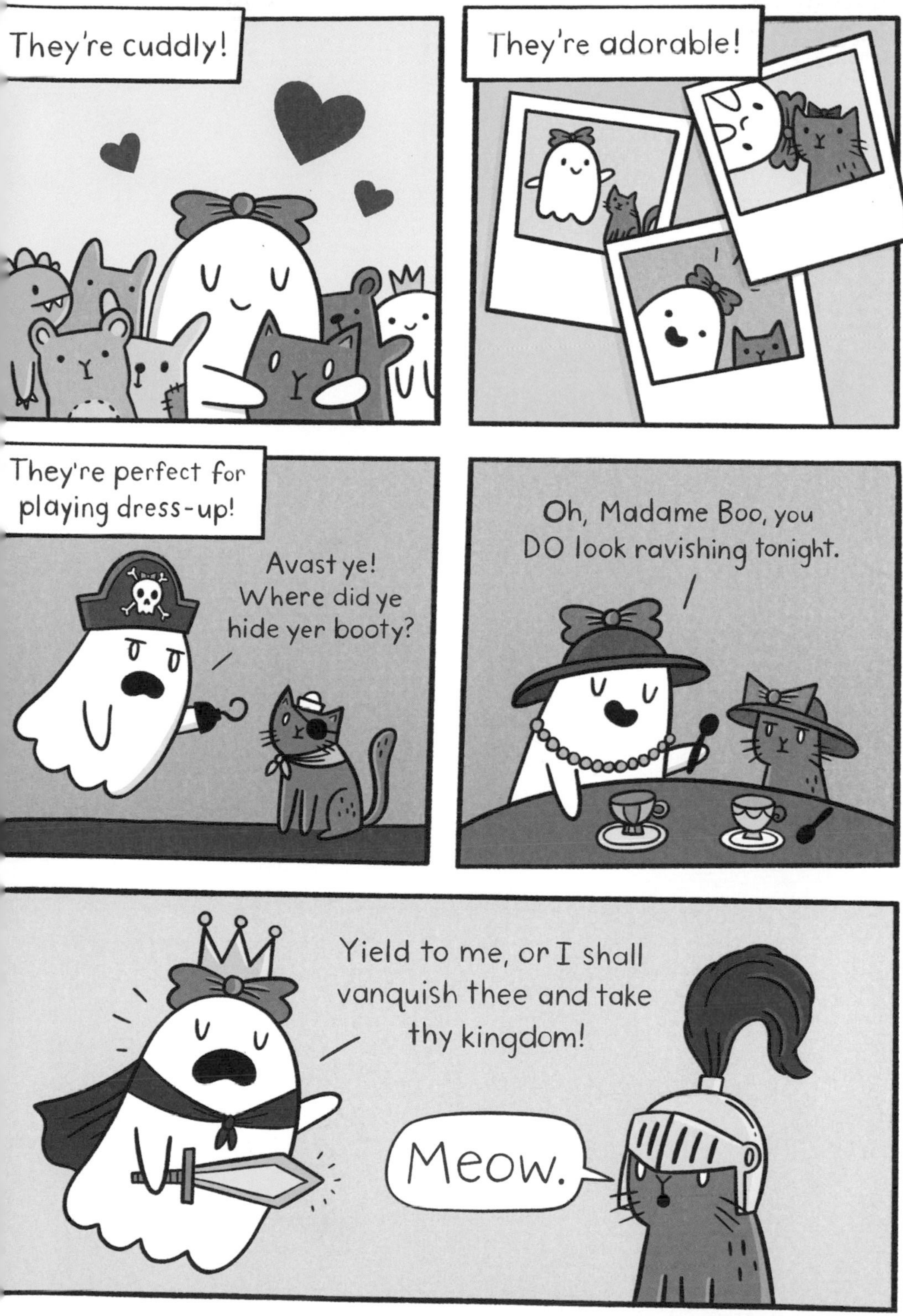

They're cuddly!
They're adorable!
They're perfect for playing dress-up!
Avast ye! Where did ye hide yer booty?
Oh, Madame Boo, you DO look ravishing tonight.
Yield to me, or I shall vanquish thee and take thy kingdom!
Meow.

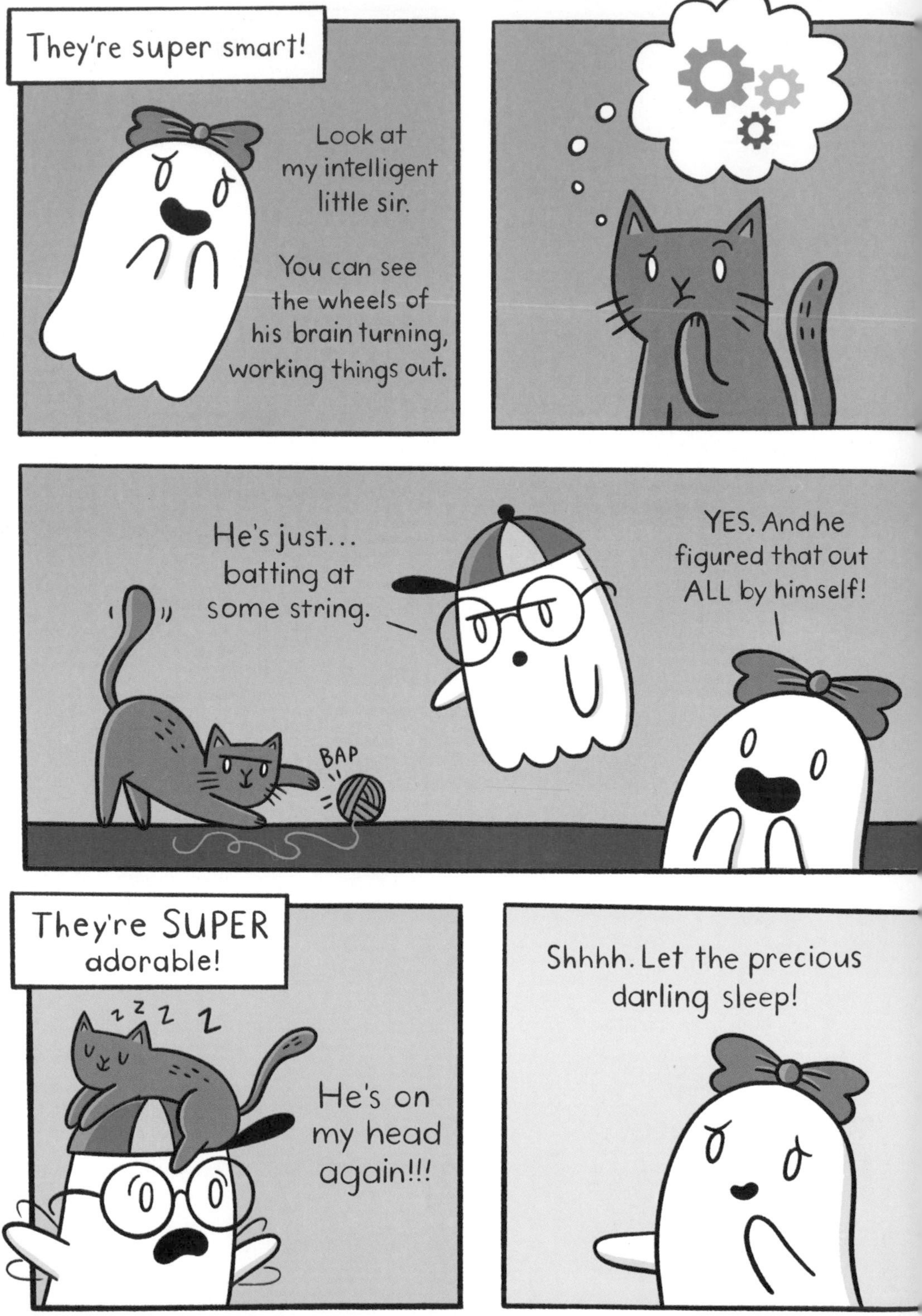
They're super smart!
Look at my intelligent little sir.
You can see the wheels of his brain turning, working things out.
He's just... batting at some string.
BAP
YES. And he figured that out ALL by himself!
They're SUPER adorable!
Z Z Z Z
He's on my head again!!!
Shhhh. Let the precious darling sleep!

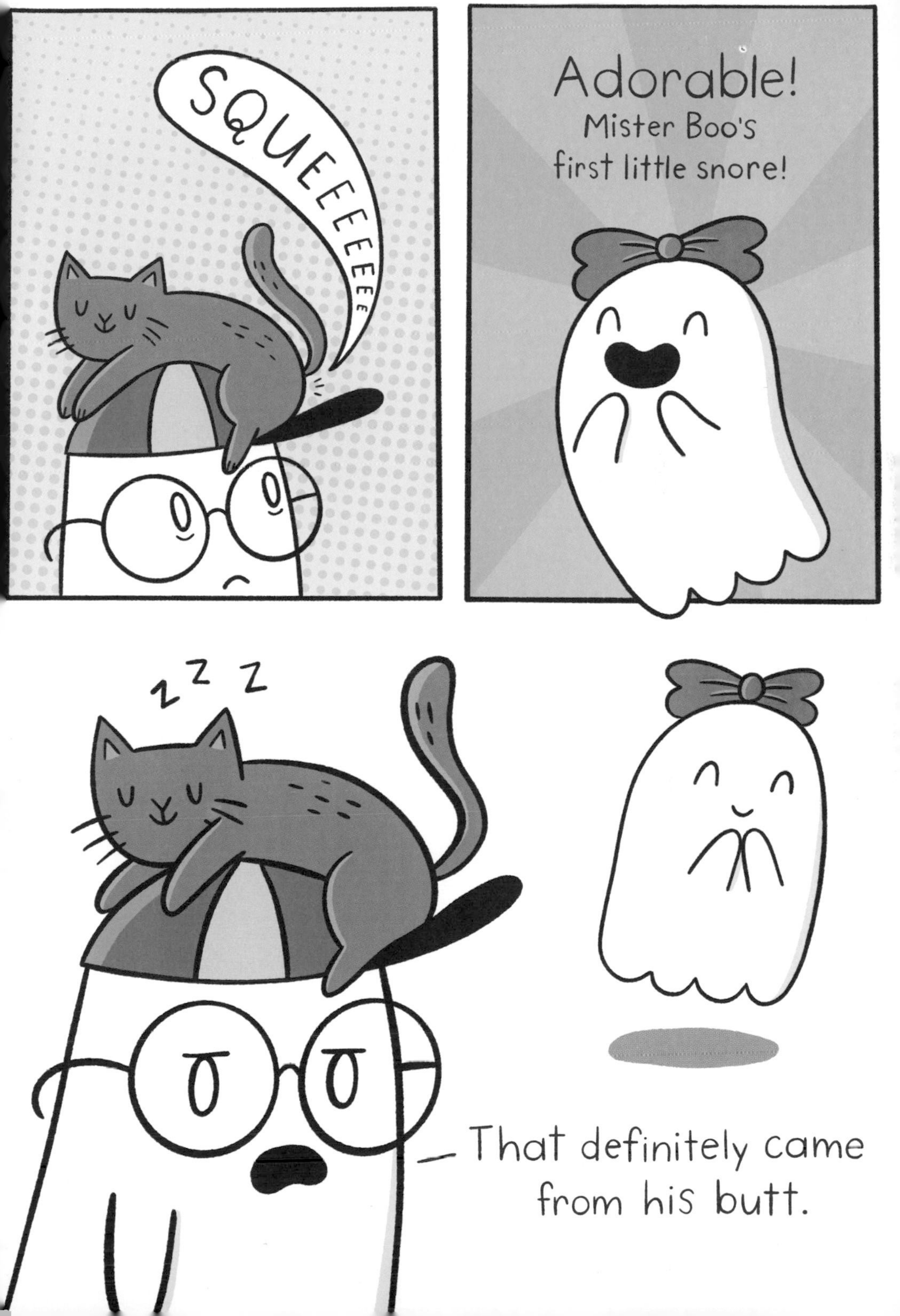

SQUEEEEEEEEEE
Adorable!
Mister Boo's
first little snore!
z z z
That definitely came
from his butt.

Catsitting

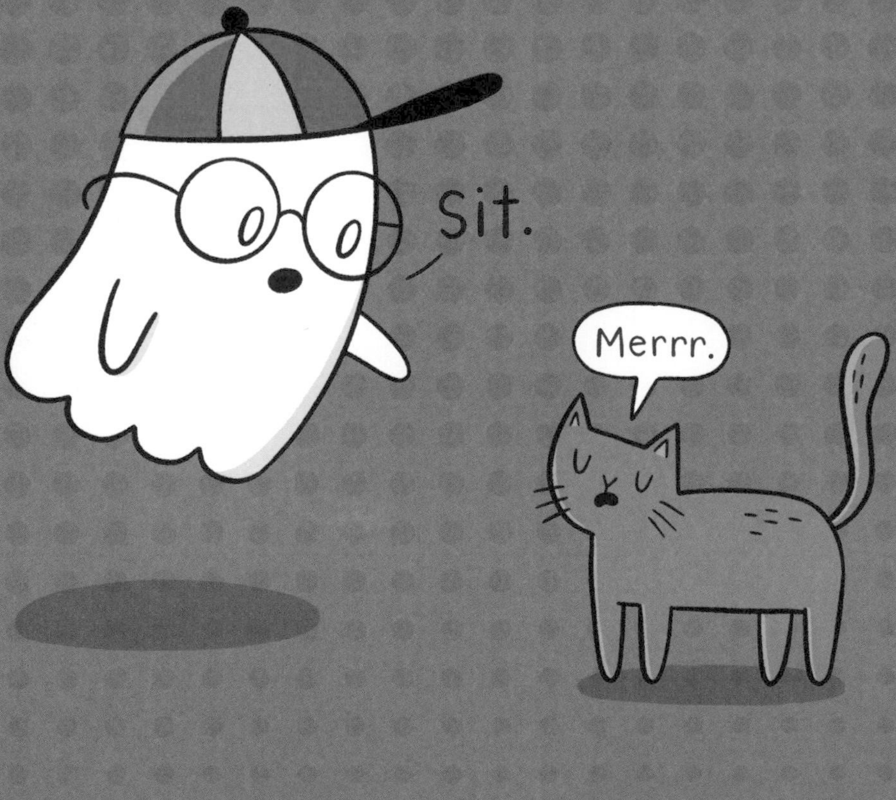
Sit.
Merrr.

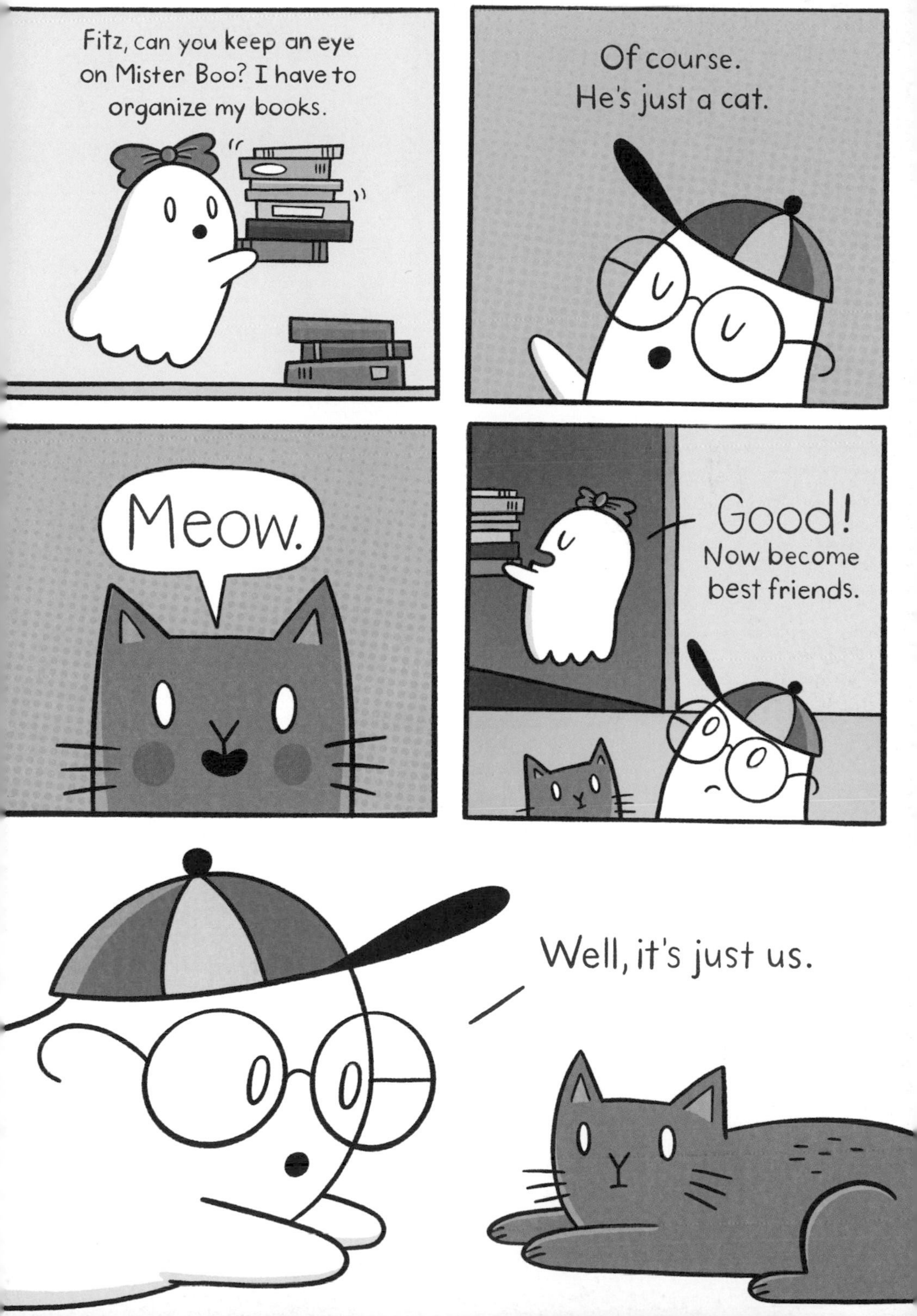
Fitz, can you keep an eye on Mister Boo? I have to organize my books.
Of course. He's just a cat.
Meow.
Good! Now become best friends.
Well, it's just us.

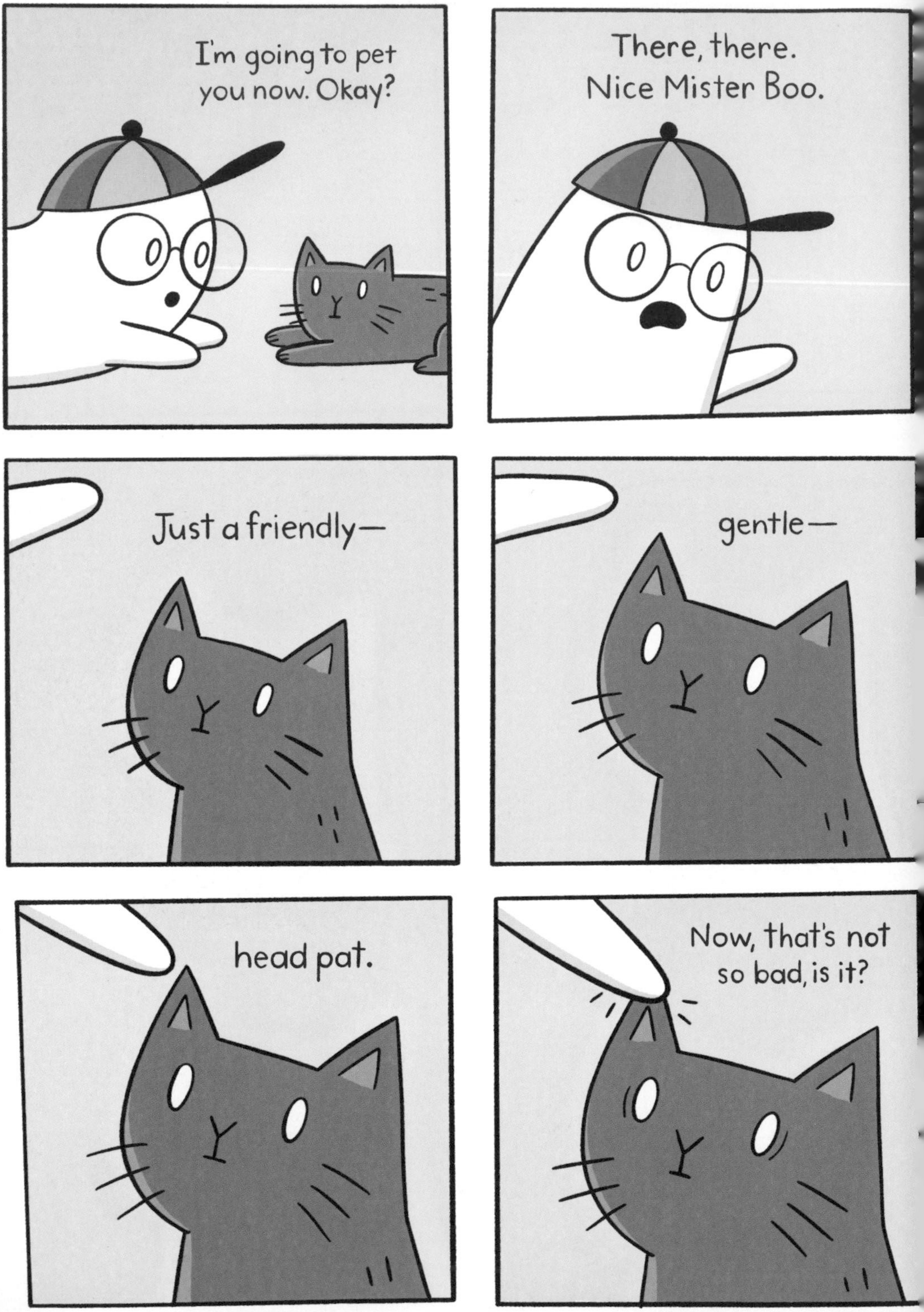
I'm going to pet you now. Okay?
There, there. Nice Mister Boo.
Just a friendly—
gentle—
head pat.
Now, that's not so bad, is it?

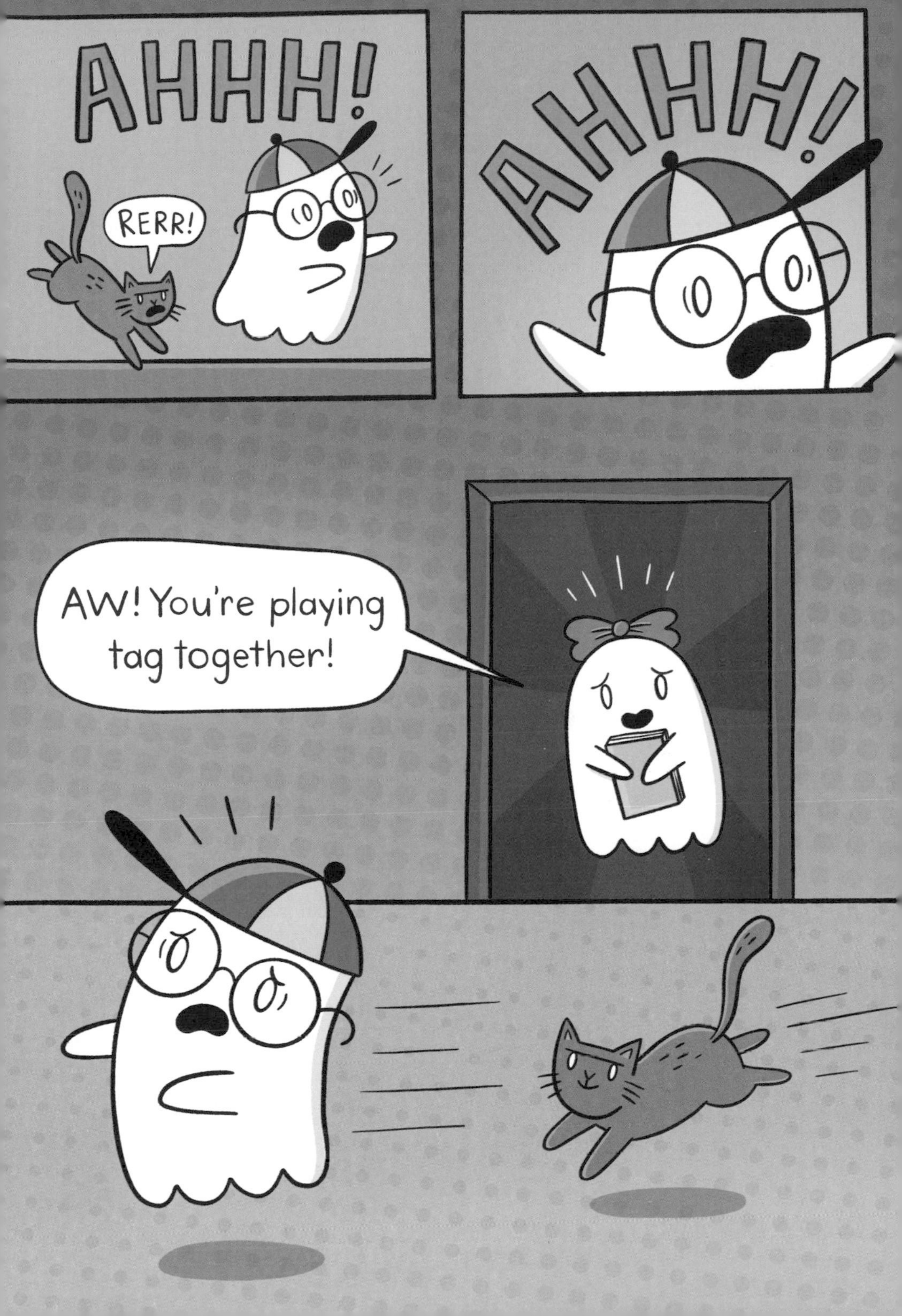
AHHH!
RERR!
AHHH!
AW! You're playing tag together!

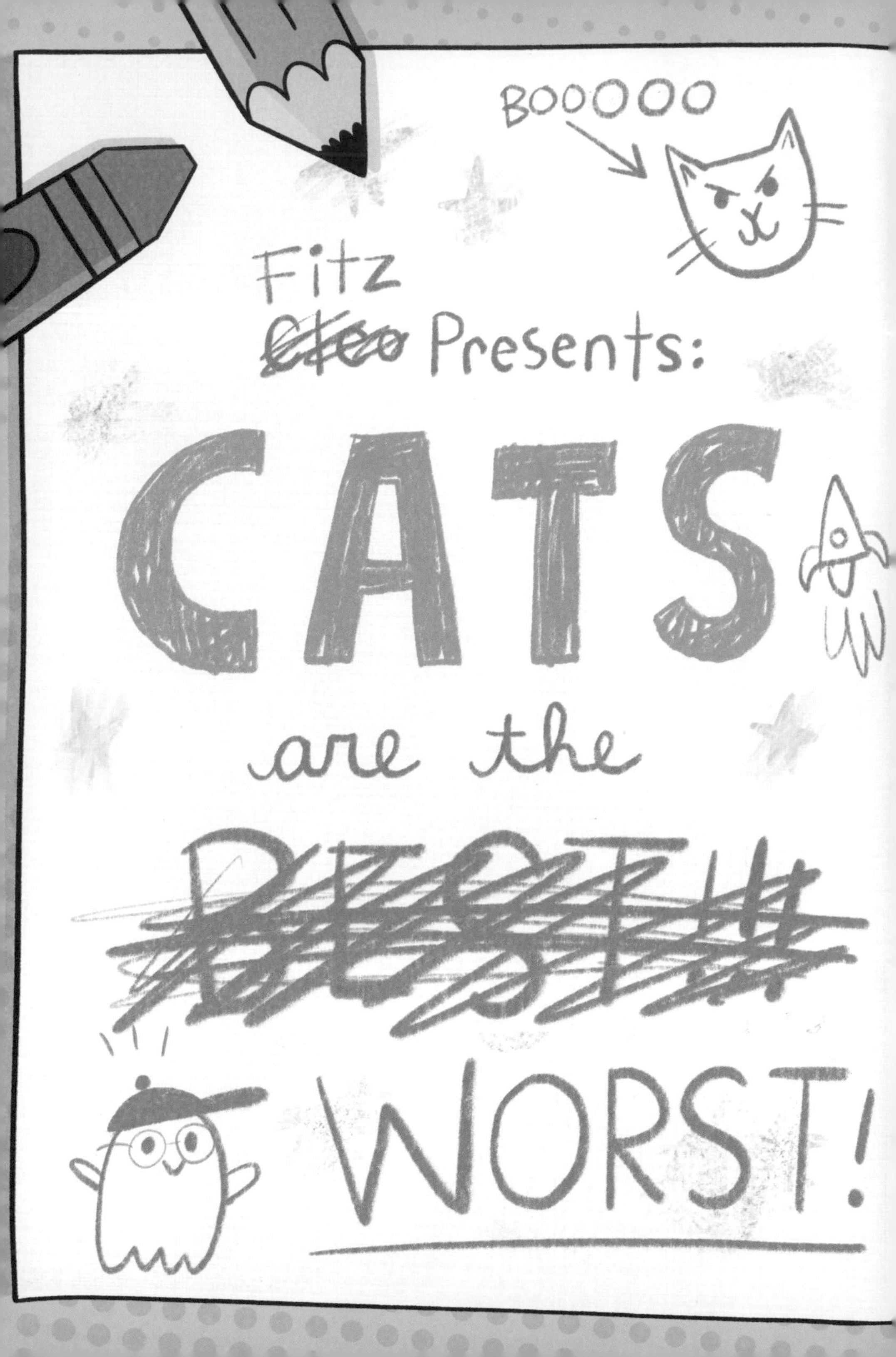
BOOOOO
Fitz
~~Cleo~~ Presents:
CATS
are the
~~BEST!!~~
WORST!

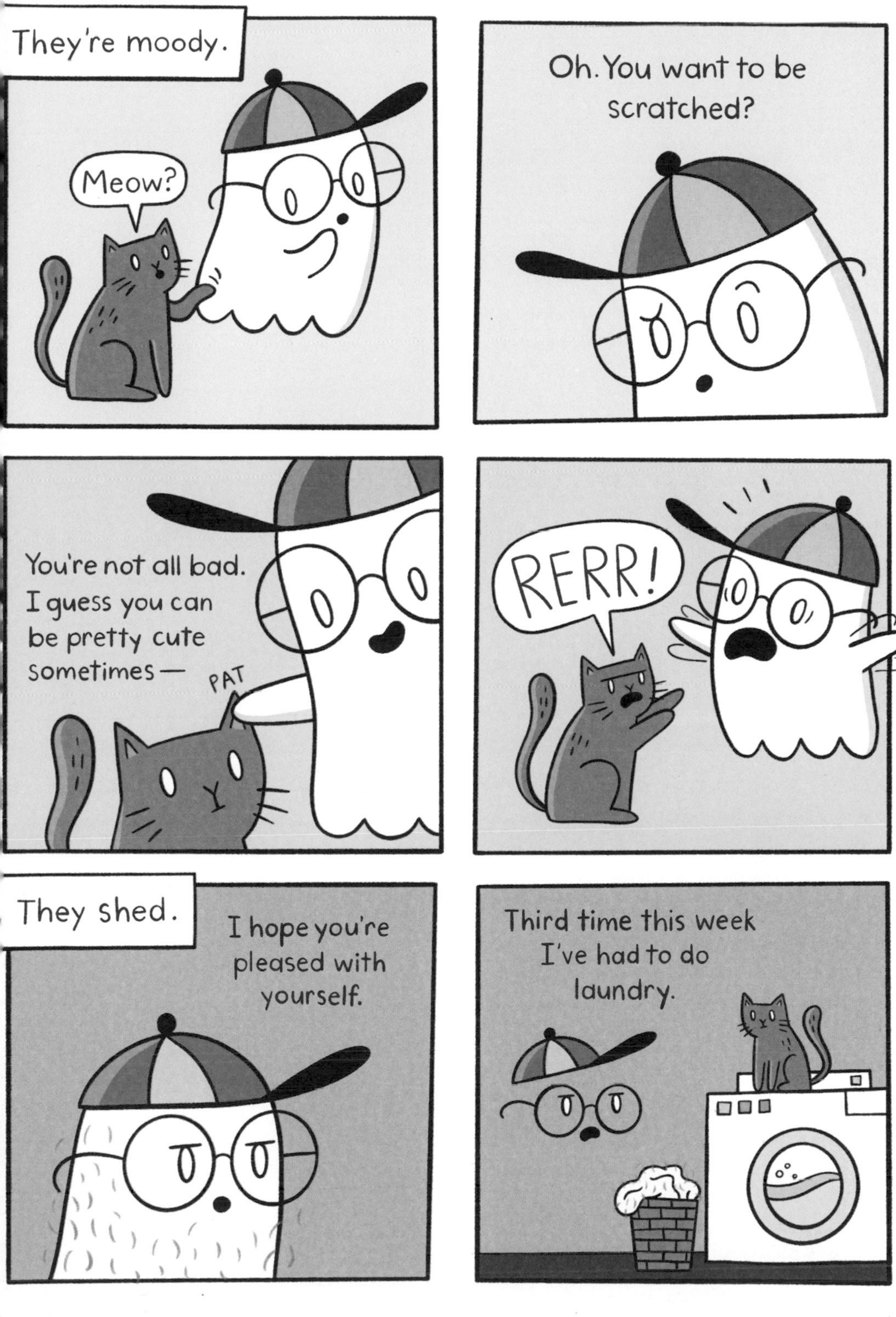
They're moody.
Meow?
Oh. You want to be scratched?
You're not all bad. I guess you can be pretty cute sometimes—
PAT
RERR!
They shed.
I hope you're pleased with yourself.
Third time this week I've had to do laundry.

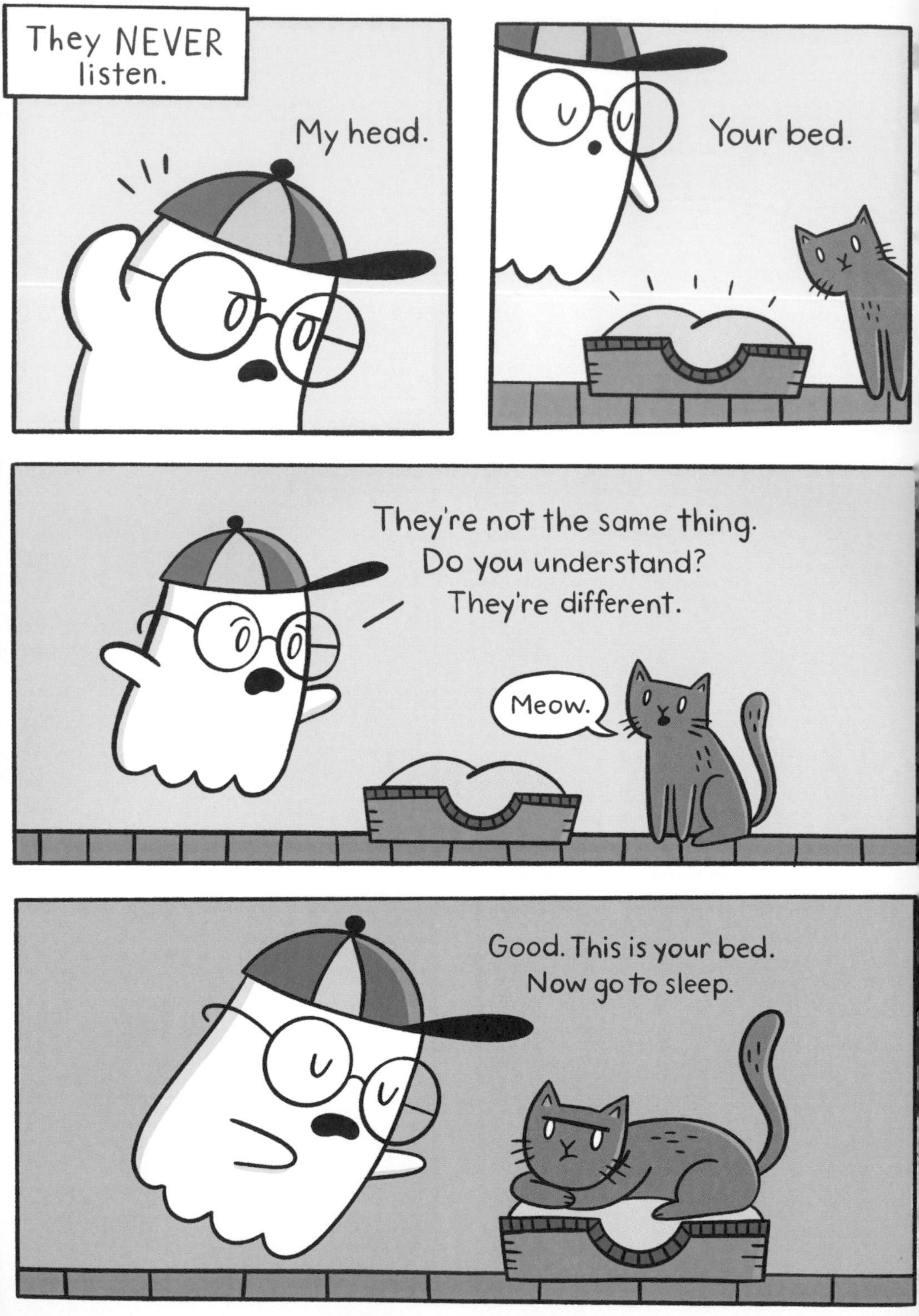
They NEVER listen.
My head.
Your bed.
They're not the same thing. Do you understand? They're different.
Meow.
Good. This is your bed. Now go to sleep.

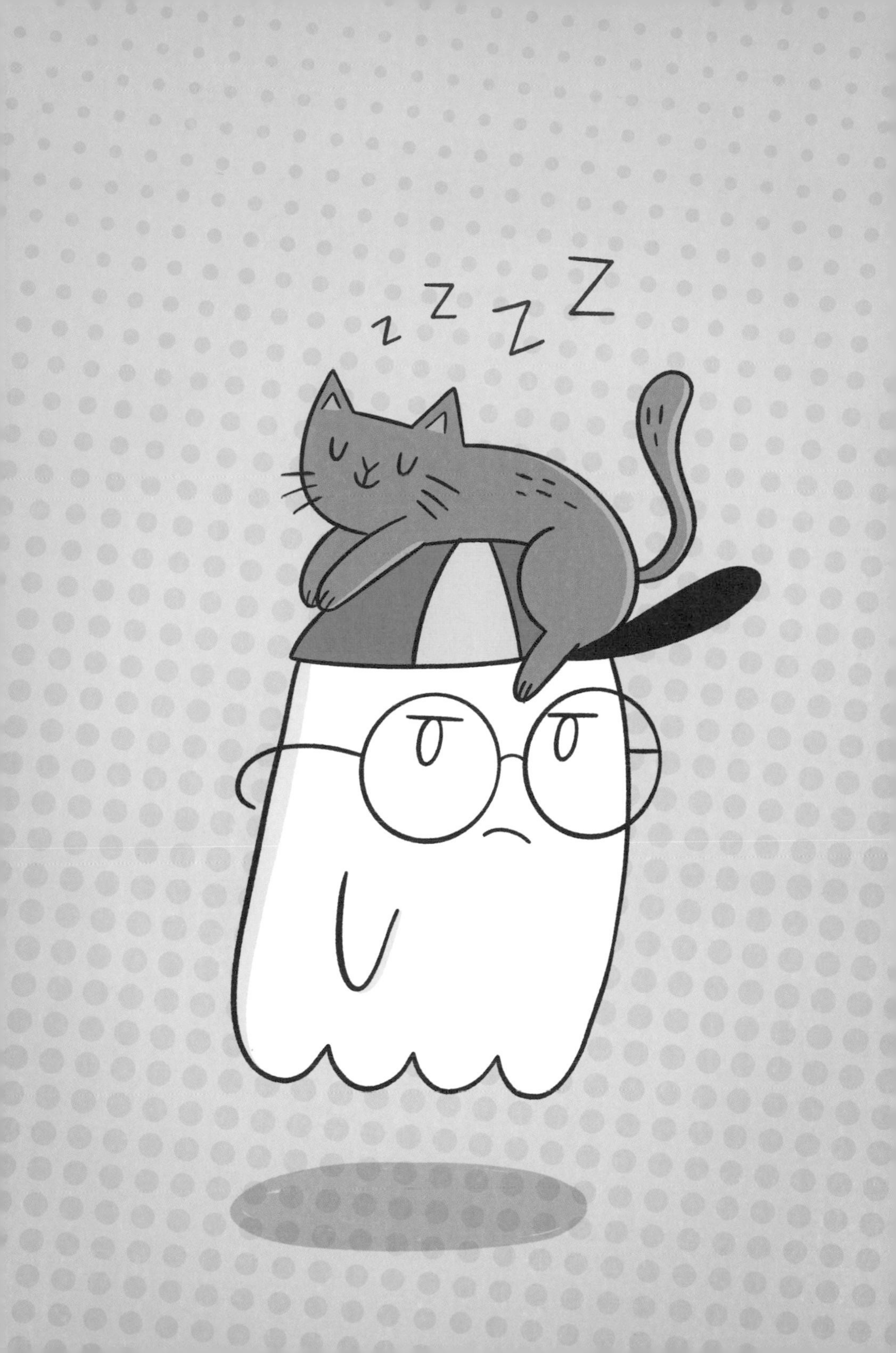
z Z Z Z

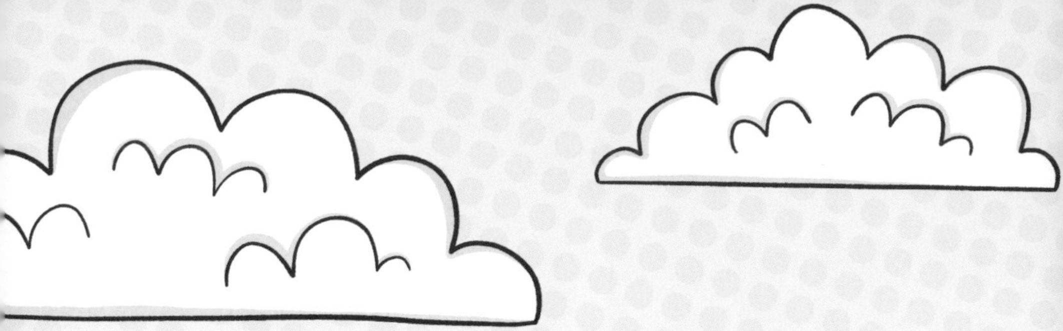

Beach Day

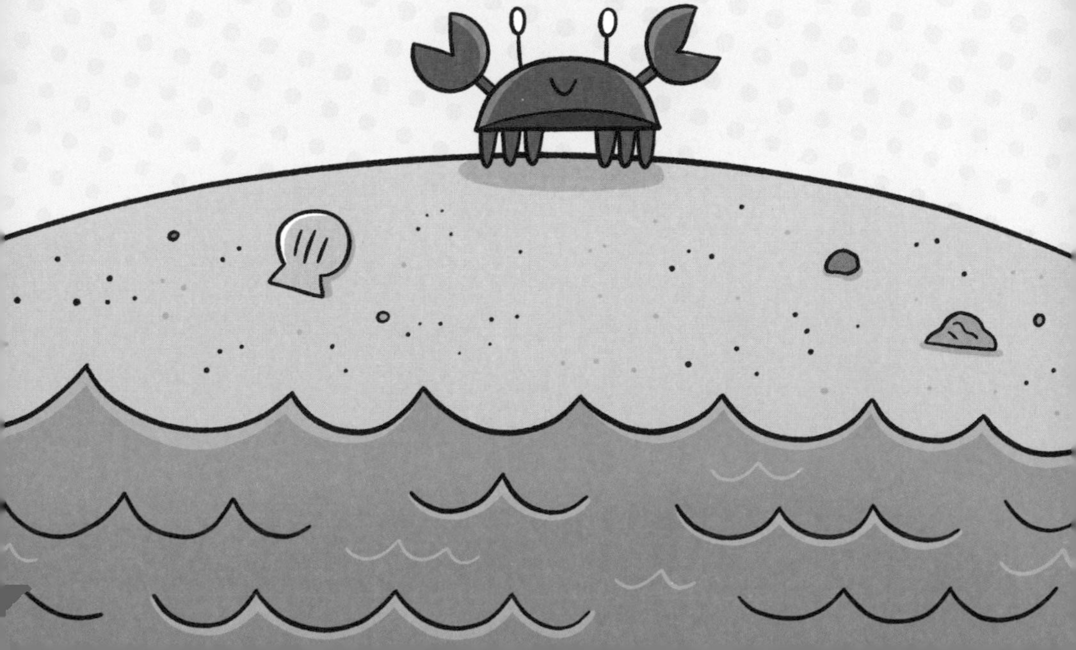

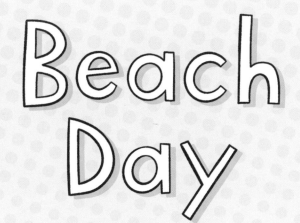

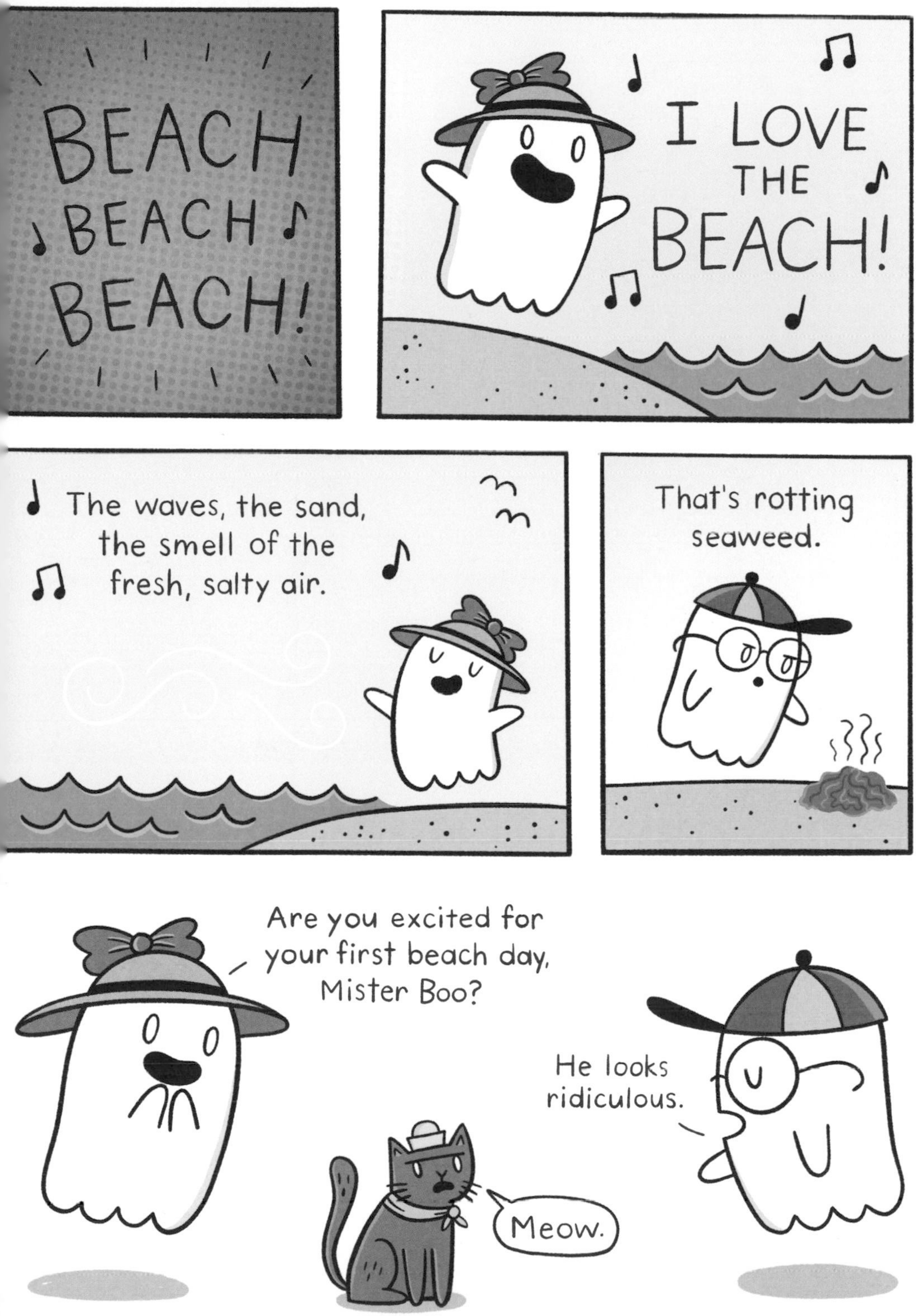
BEACH
BEACH
BEACH!
I LOVE THE BEACH!
The waves, the sand, the smell of the fresh, salty air.
That's rotting seaweed.
Are you excited for your first beach day, Mister Boo?
He looks ridiculous.
Meow.

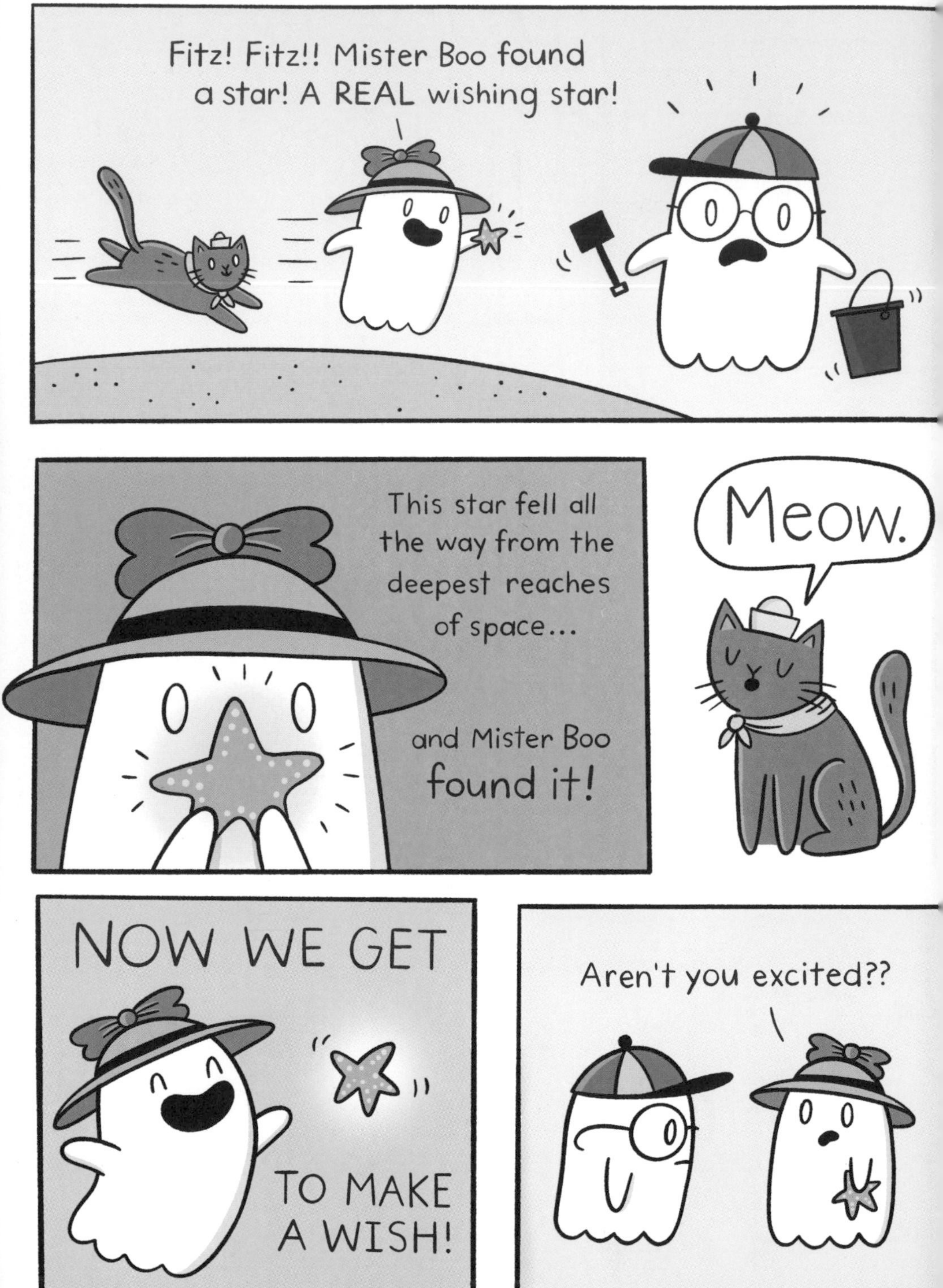

Fitz! Fitz!! Mister Boo found a star! A REAL wishing star!
This star fell all the way from the deepest reaches of space...
and Mister Boo found it!
Meow.
NOW WE GET
TO MAKE A WISH!
Aren't you excited??

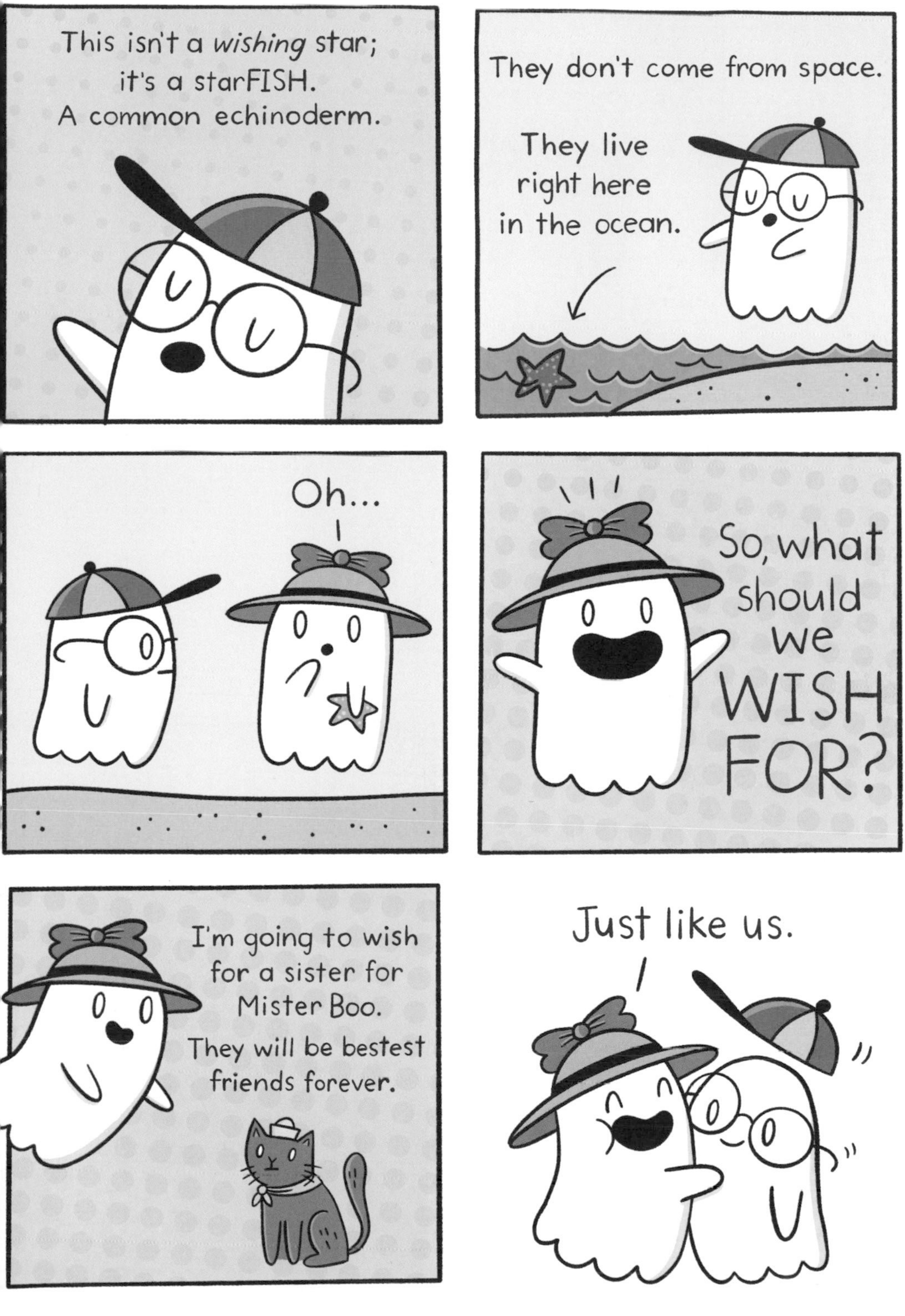
This isn't a *wishing* star; it's a starFISH. A common echinoderm.
They don't come from space.
They live right here in the ocean.
Oh...
So, what should we WISH FOR?
I'm going to wish for a sister for Mister Boo. They will be bestest friends forever.
Just like us.

We ALL Scream

ICE CREAM
ICE CREAM!!

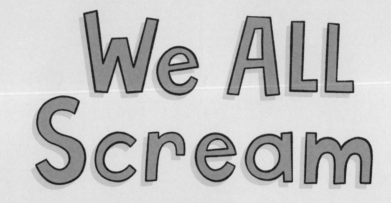

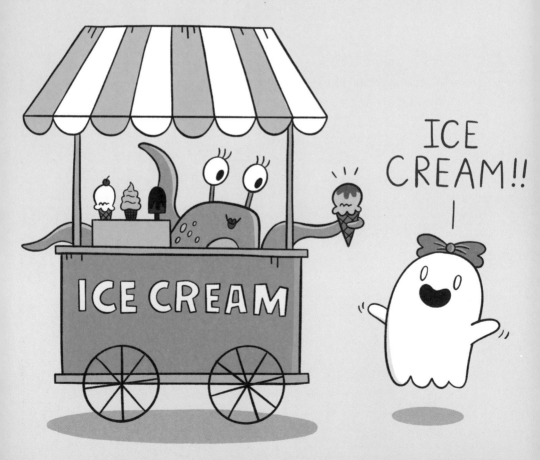

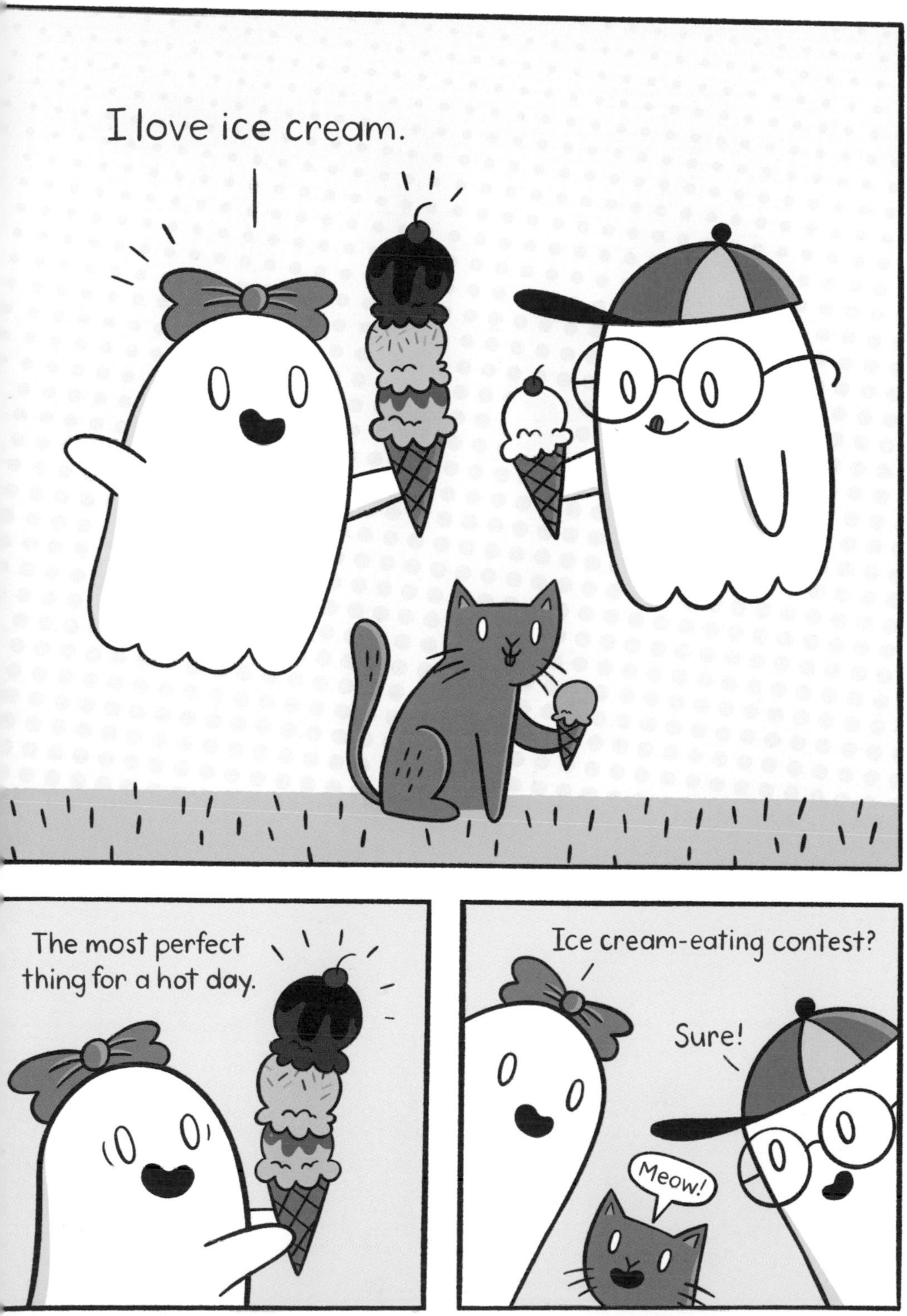
I love ice cream.
The most perfect thing for a hot day.
Ice cream-eating contest?
Sure!
Meow!

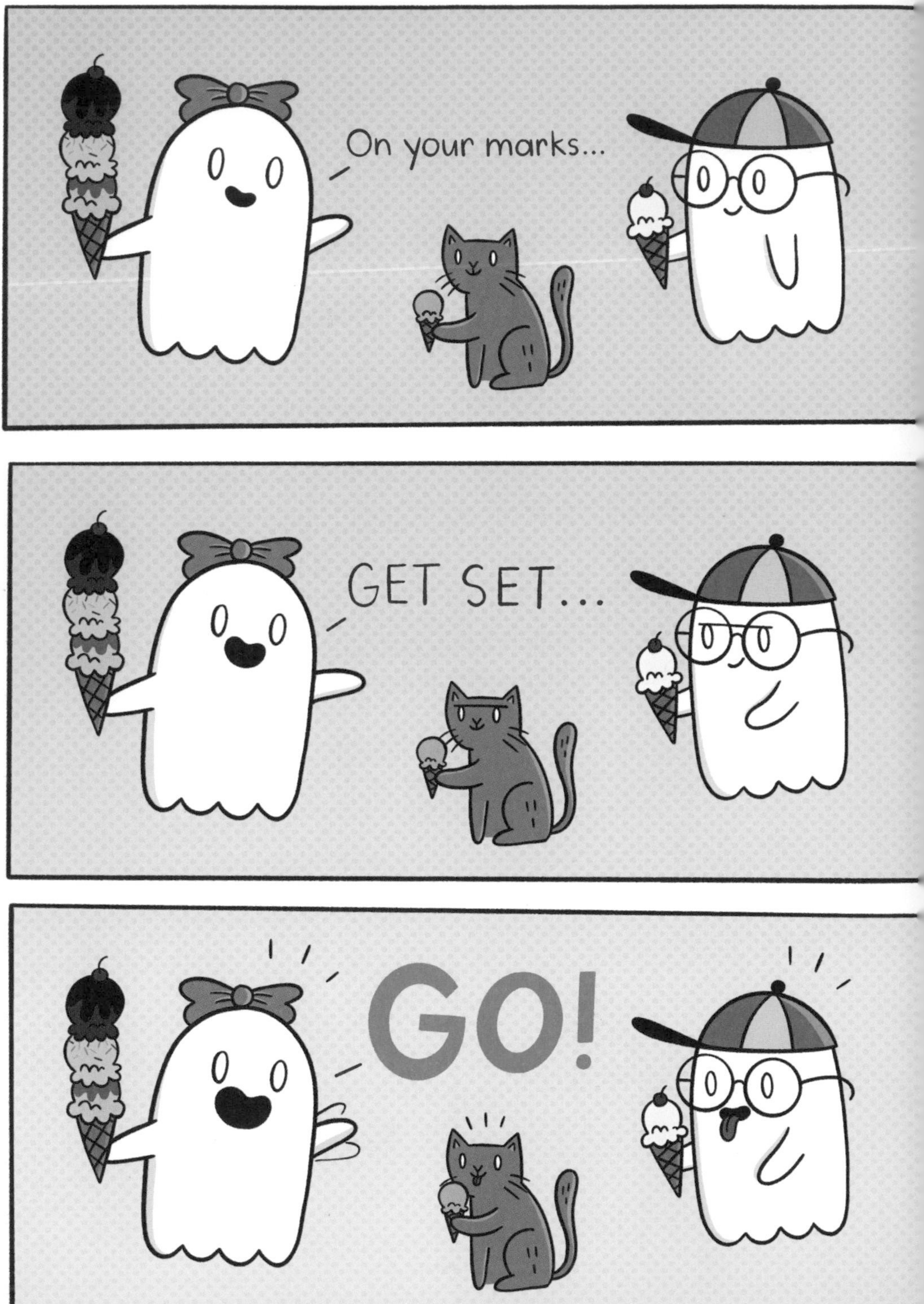

On your marks...
GET SET...
GO!

LICK LICK
CHOMP LICK

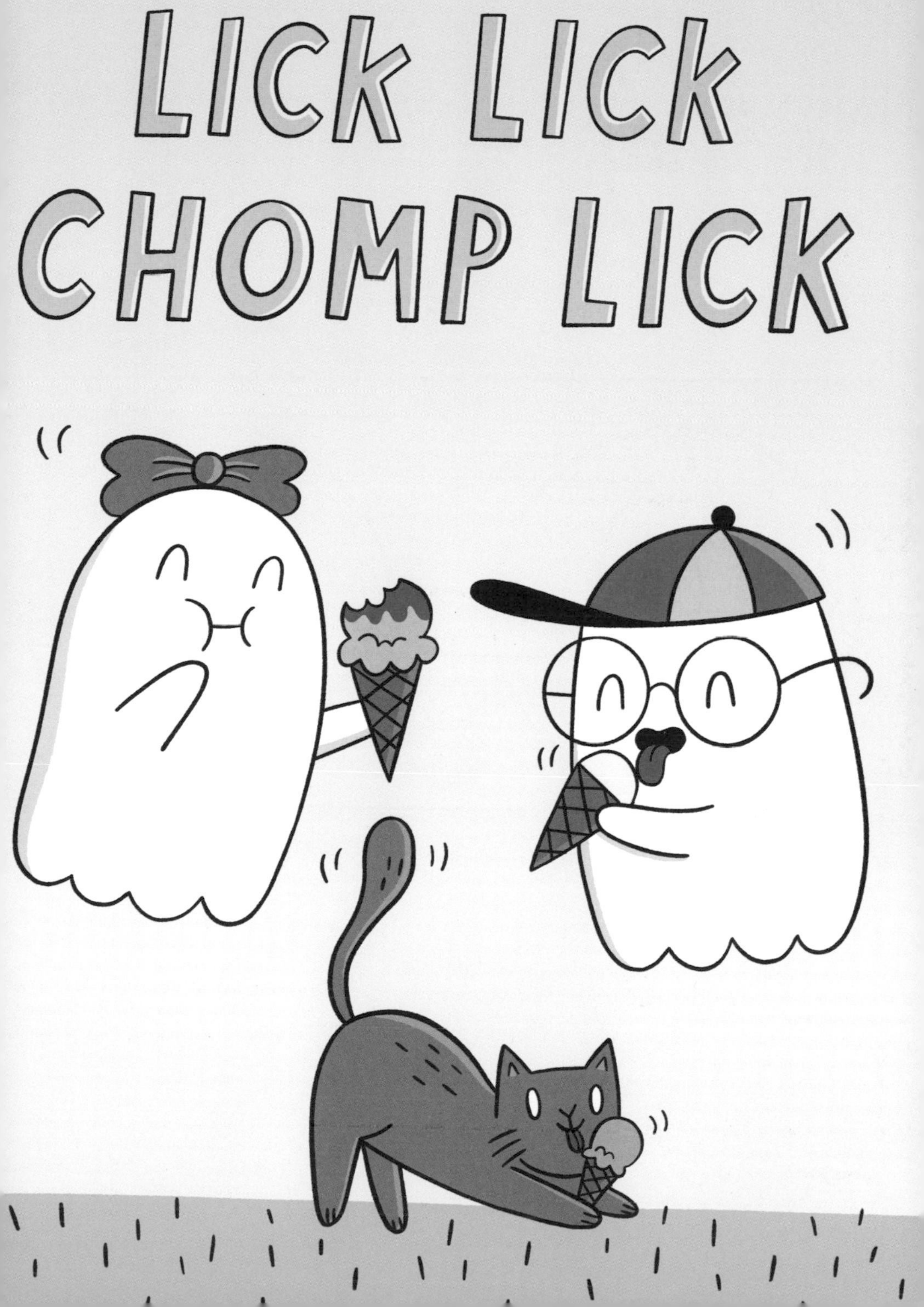

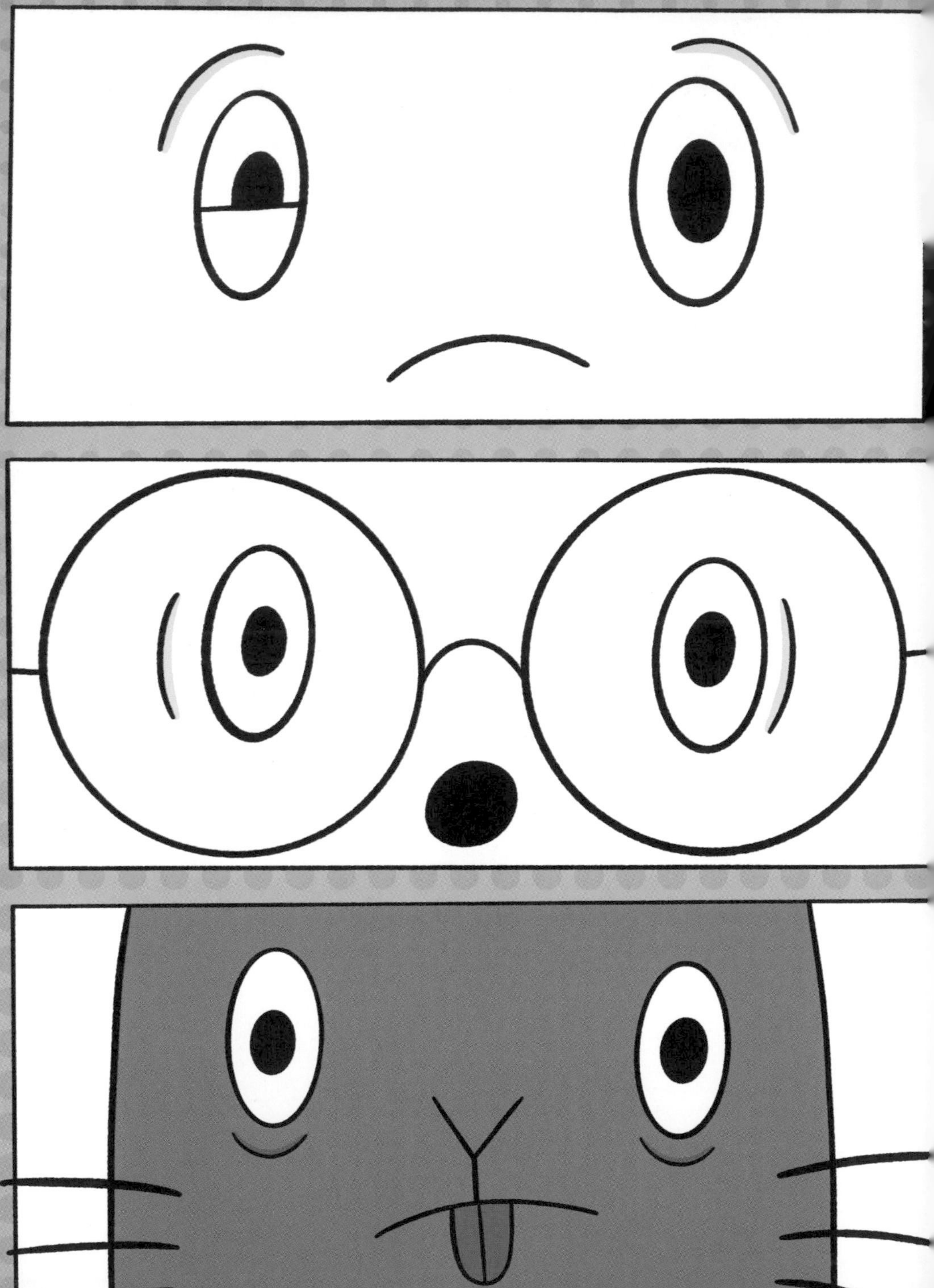

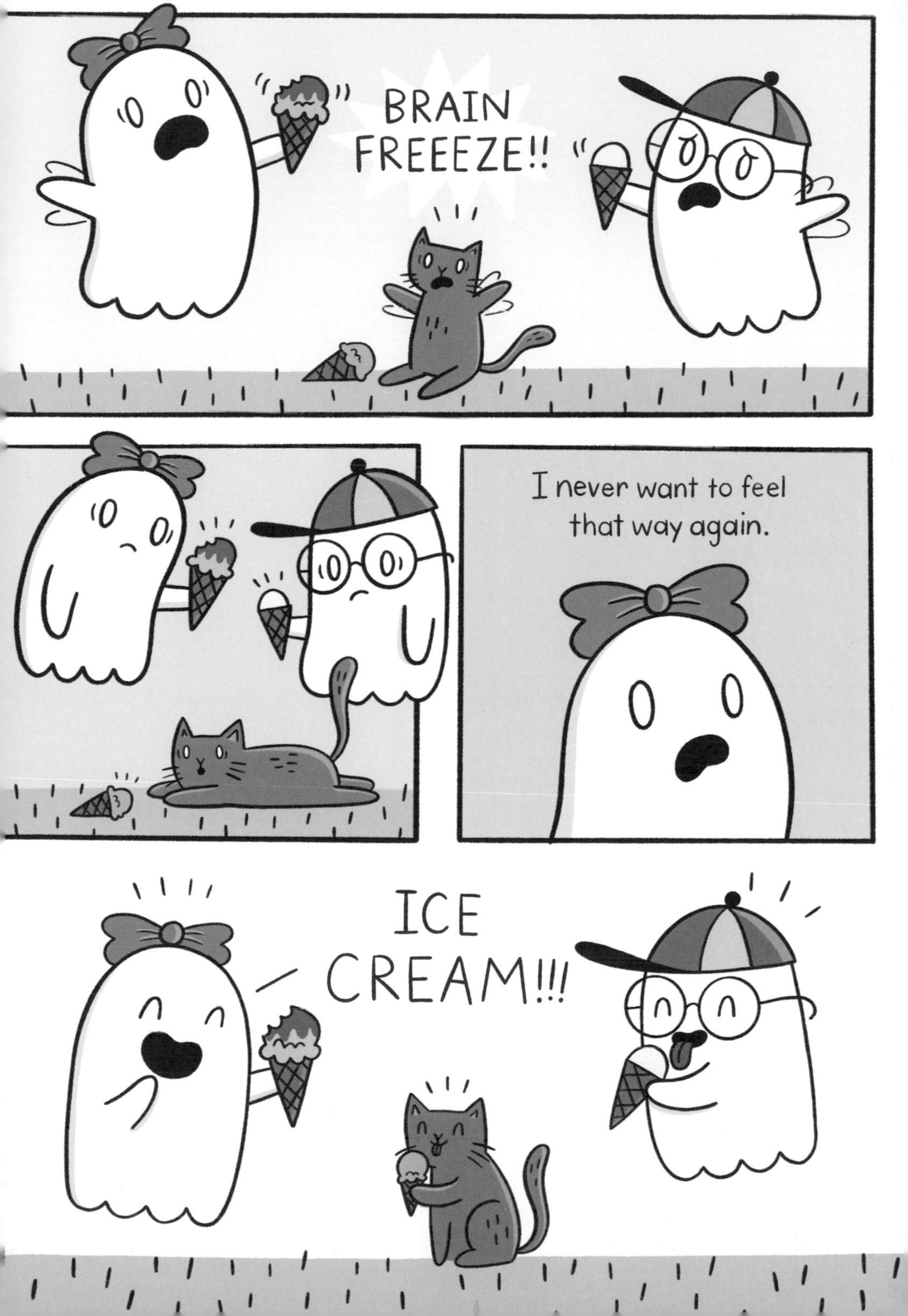
BRAIN FREEEZE!!
I never want to feel that way again.
ICE CREAM!!!

Paper Planes

For the loop-de-loop
world record,
she needs...
SEVEN LOOPS.

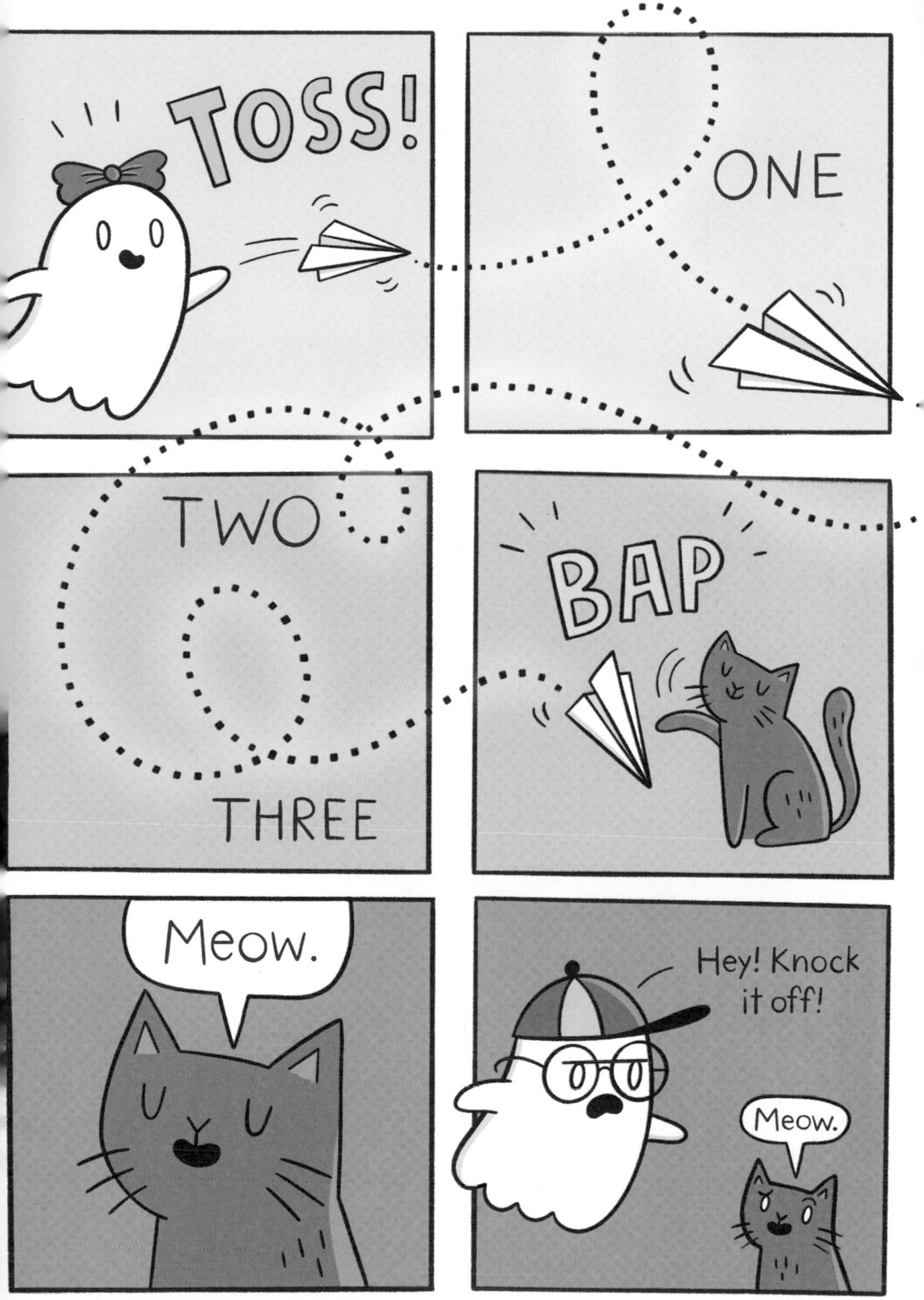
TOSS!
ONE
TWO
THREE
BAP
Meow.
Hey! Knock it off!
Meow.

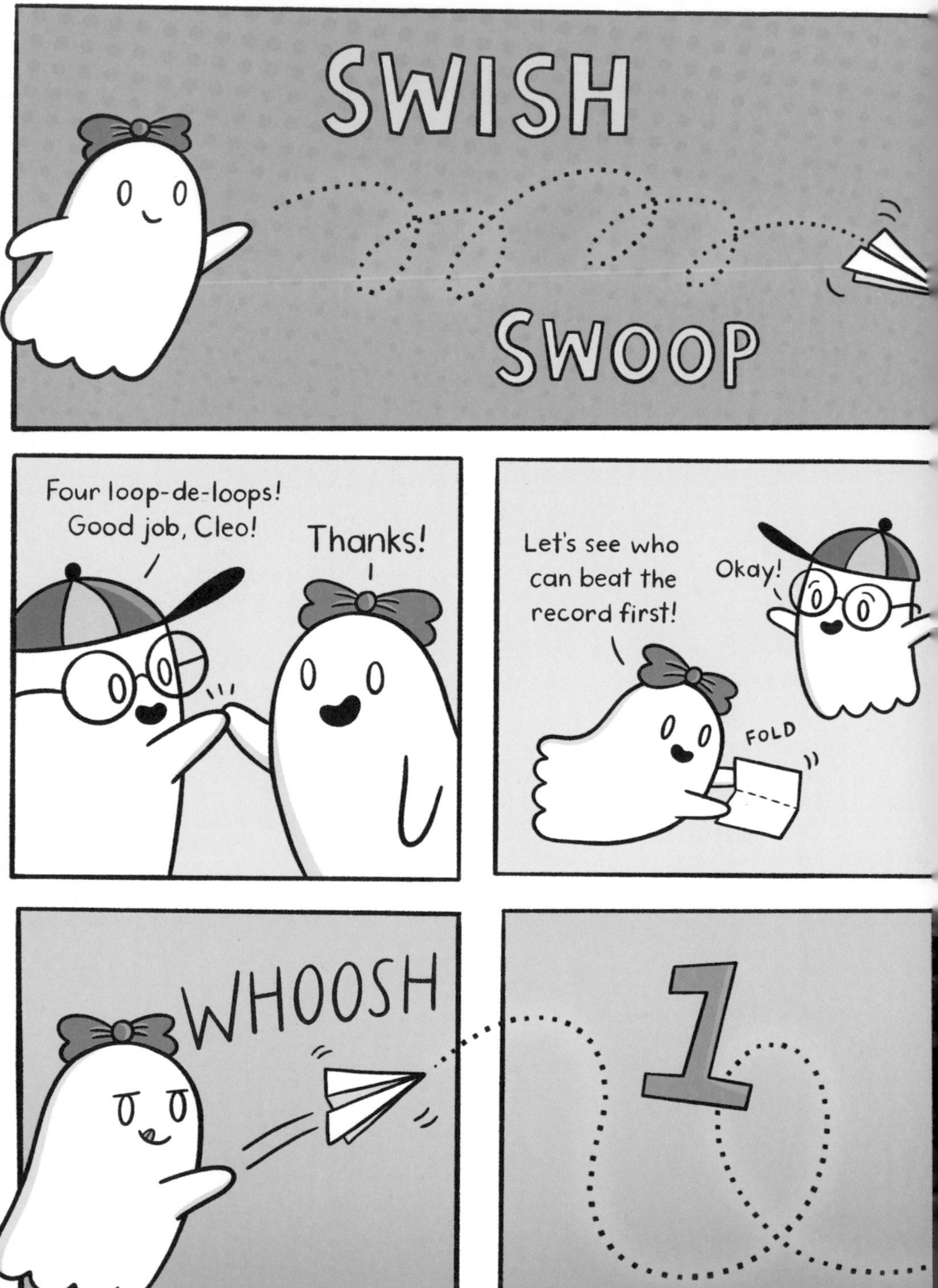
SWISH
SWOOP
Four loop-de-loops! Good job, Cleo!
Thanks!
Let's see who can beat the record first!
Okay!
FOLD
WHOOSH
1

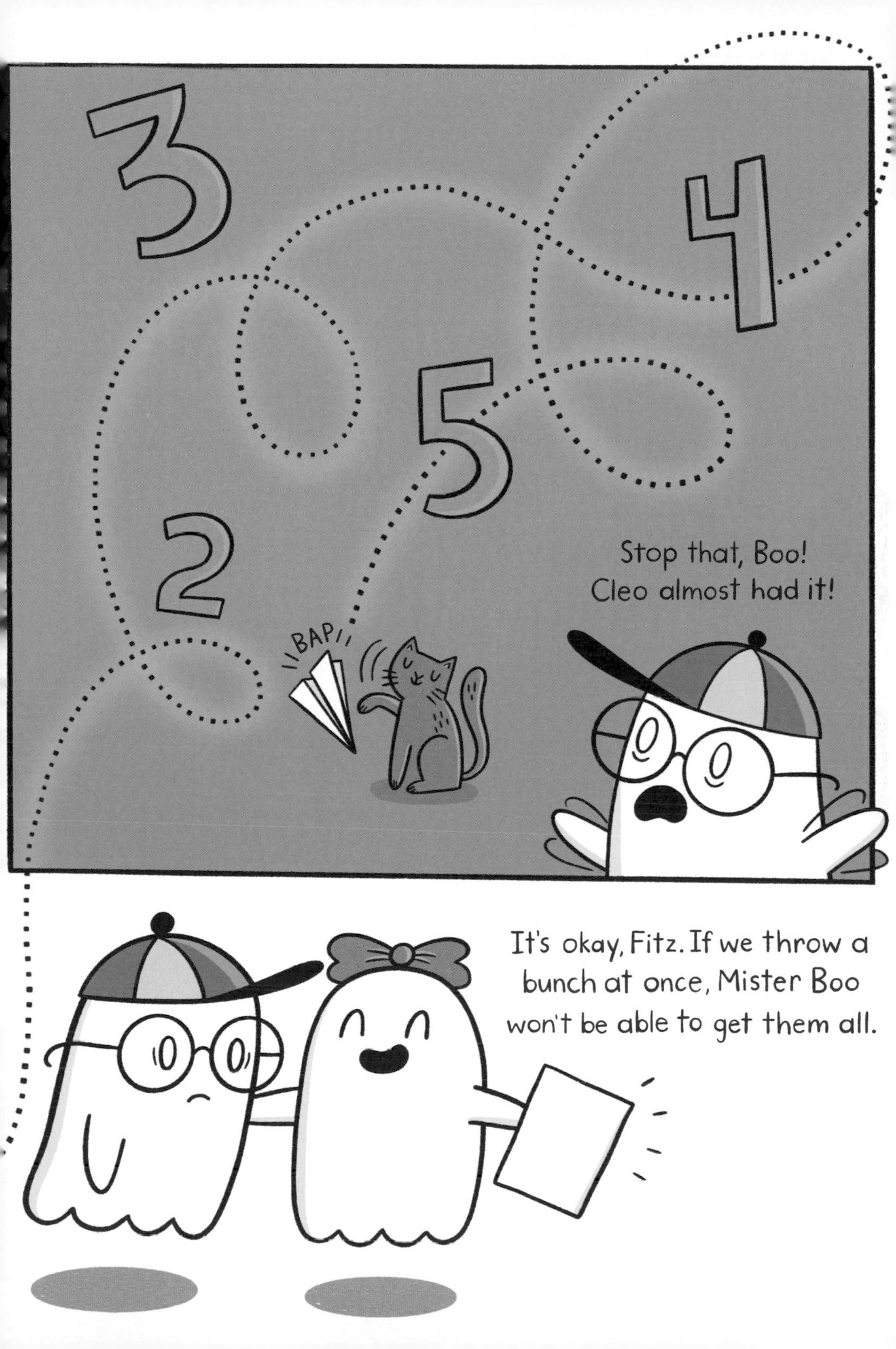
3
4
5
2
BAP
Stop that, Boo!
Cleo almost had it!
It's okay, Fitz. If we throw a
bunch at once, Mister Boo
won't be able to get them all.

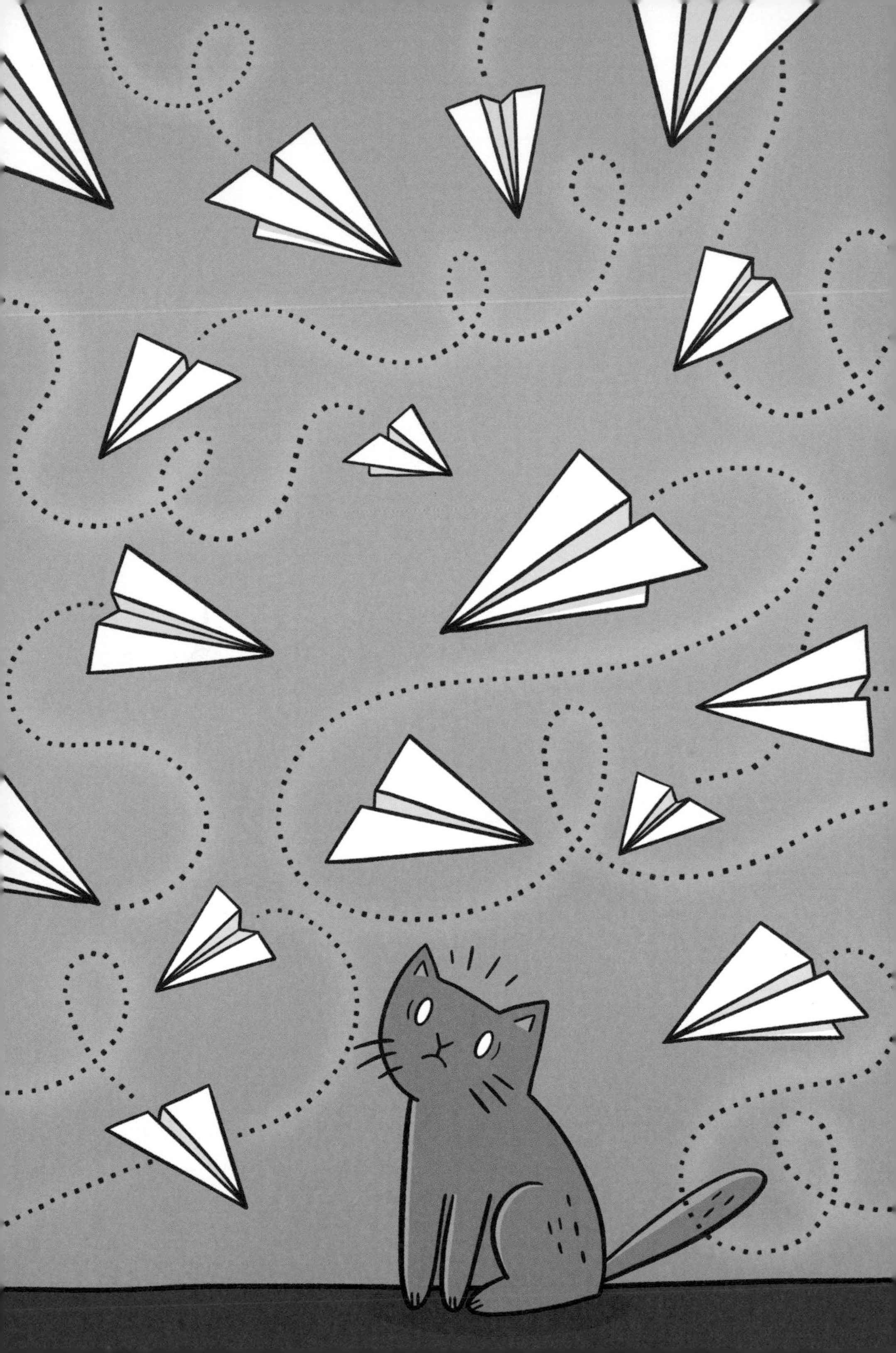

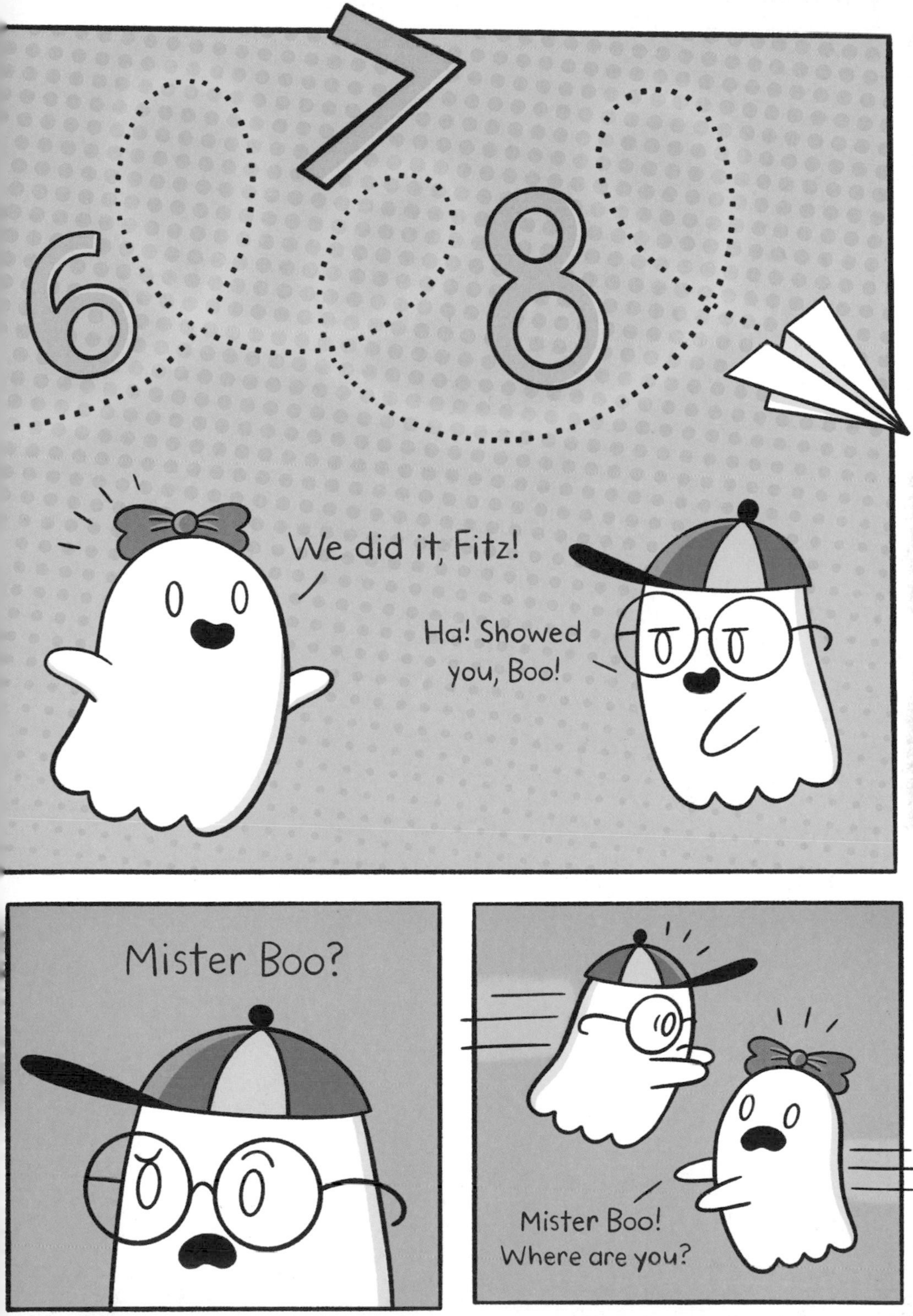

6
7
8
We did it, Fitz!
Ha! Showed you, Boo!
Mister Boo?
Mister Boo! Where are you?

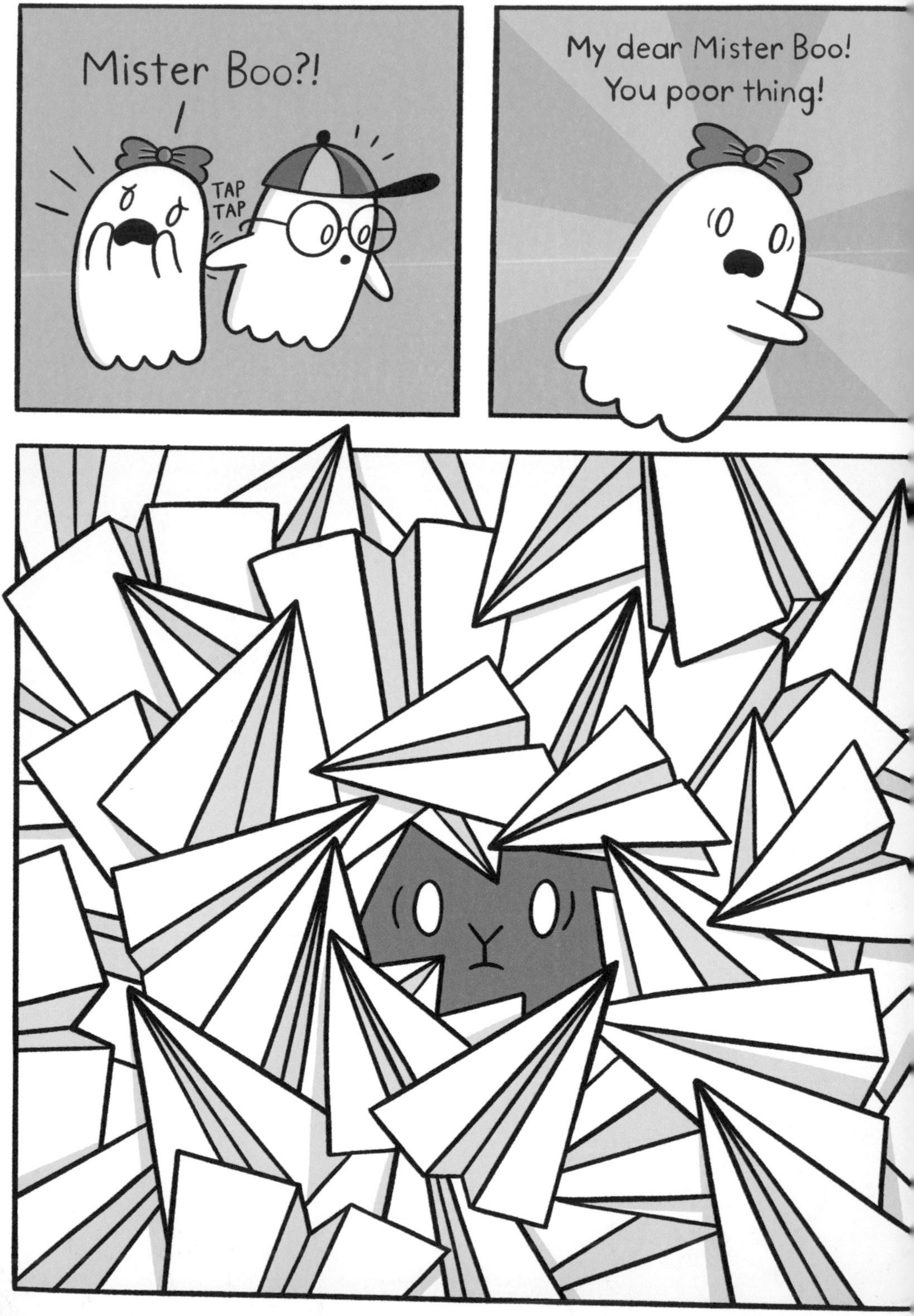
Mister Boo?!
TAP
TAP
My dear Mister Boo!
You poor thing!

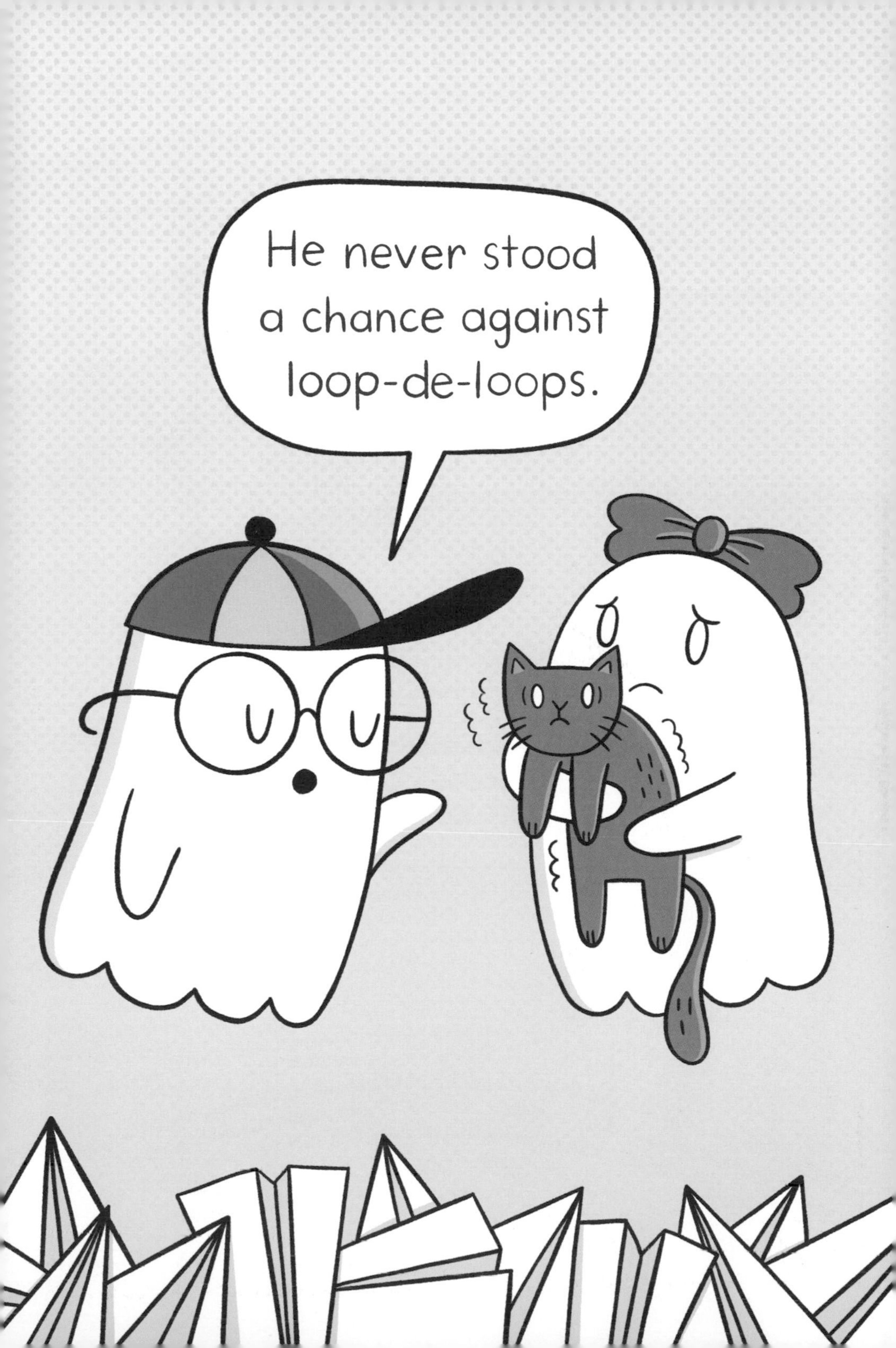
He never stood a chance against loop-de-loops.

String Theory

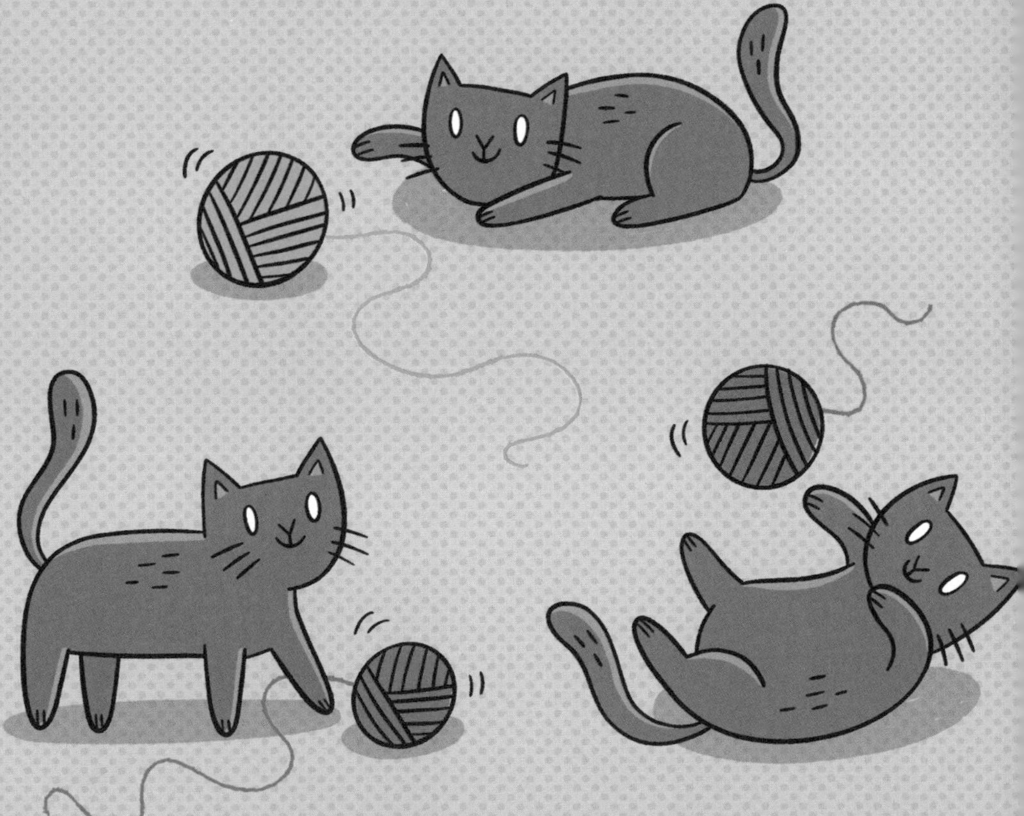

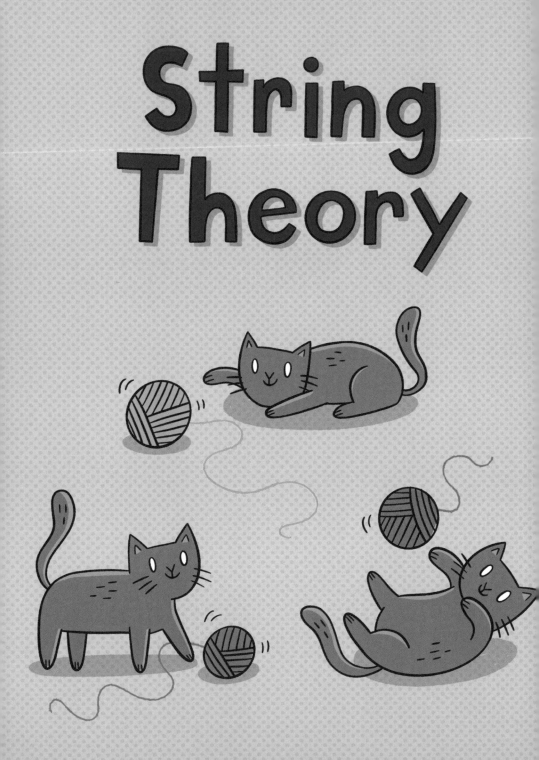

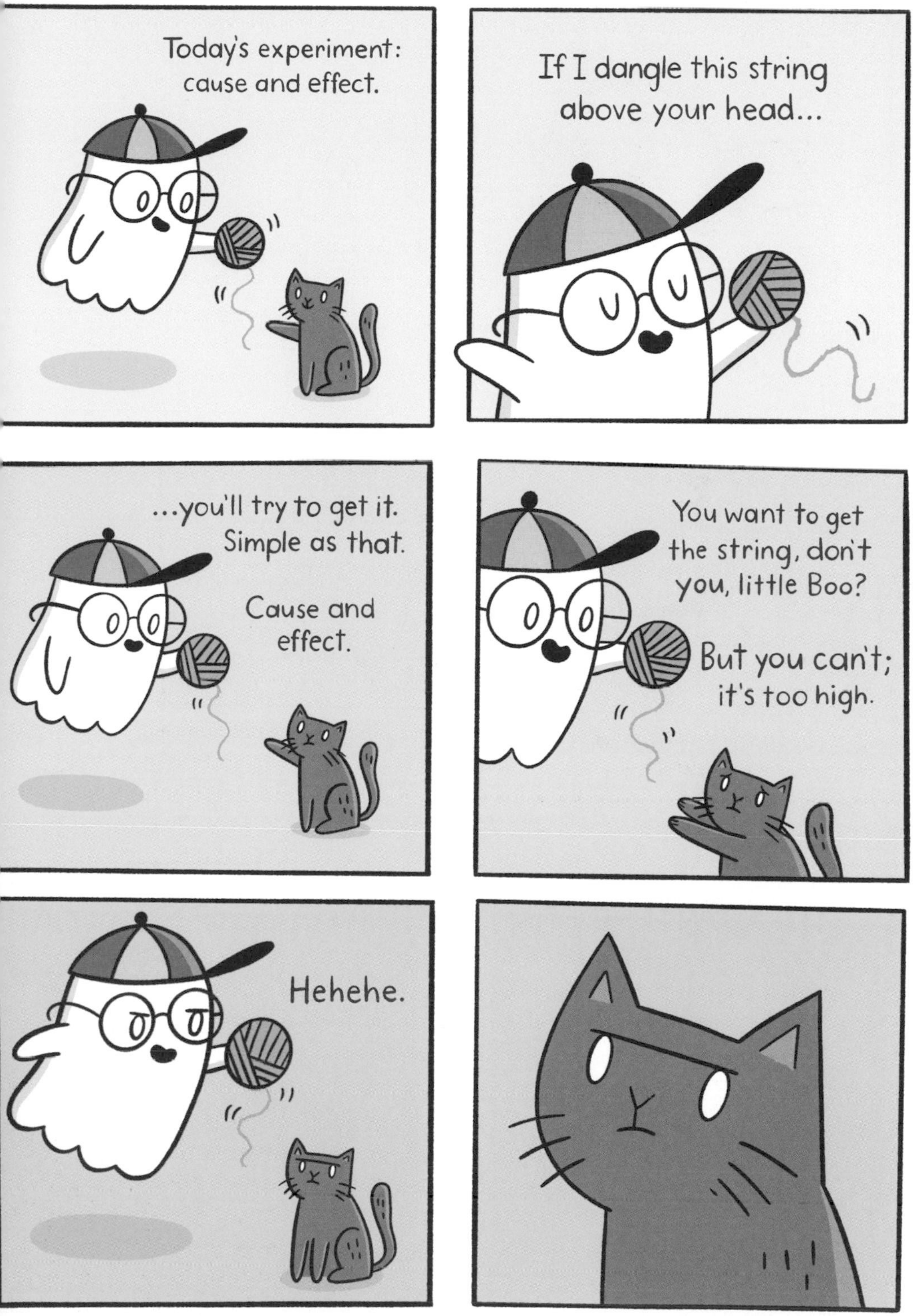
Today's experiment:
cause and effect.
If I dangle this string
above your head...
...you'll try to get it.
Simple as that.
Cause and
effect.
You want to get
the string, don't
you, little Boo?
But you can't;
it's too high.
Hehehe.

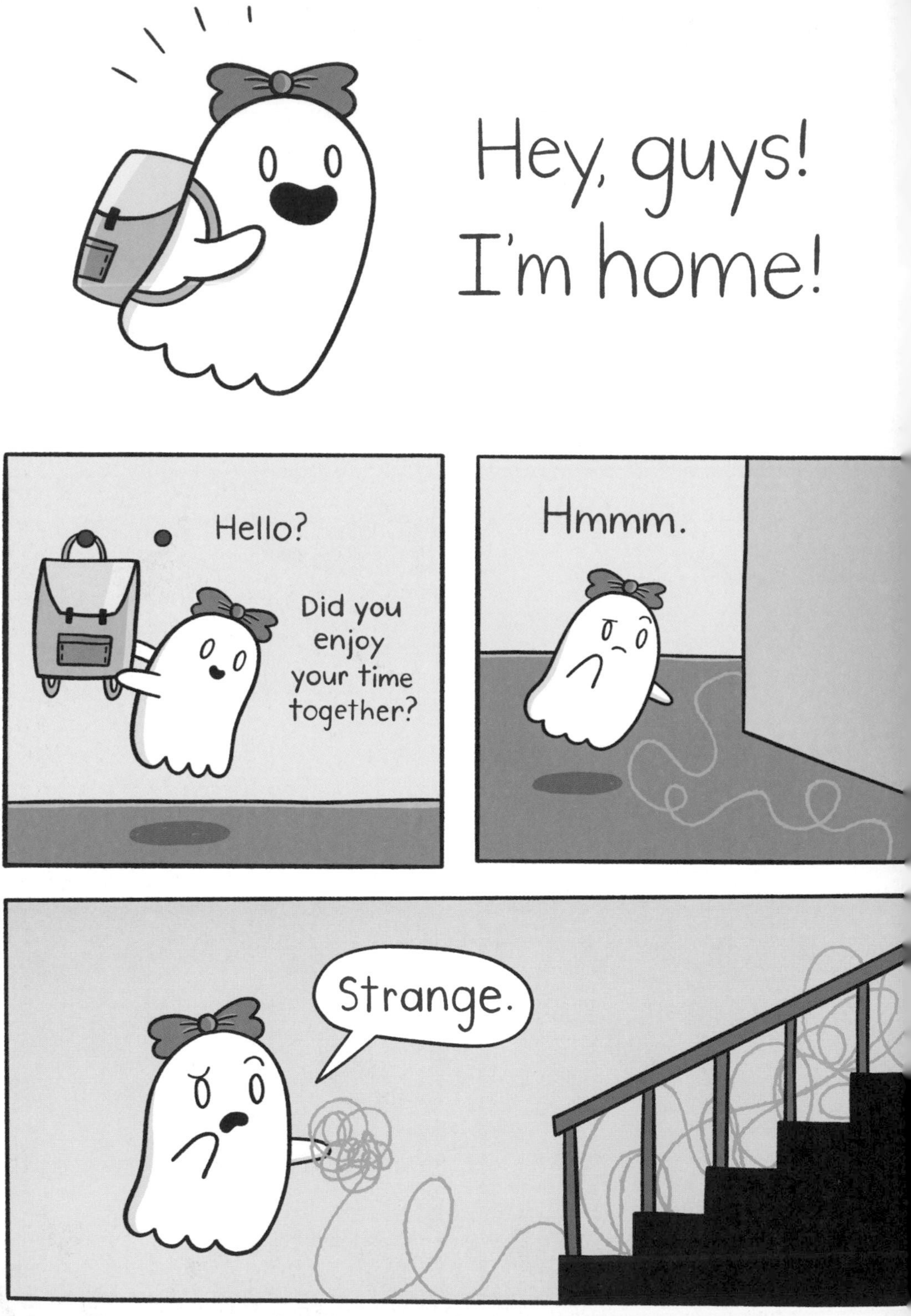
Hey, guys! I'm home!
Hello?
Did you enjoy your time together?
Hmmm.
Strange.

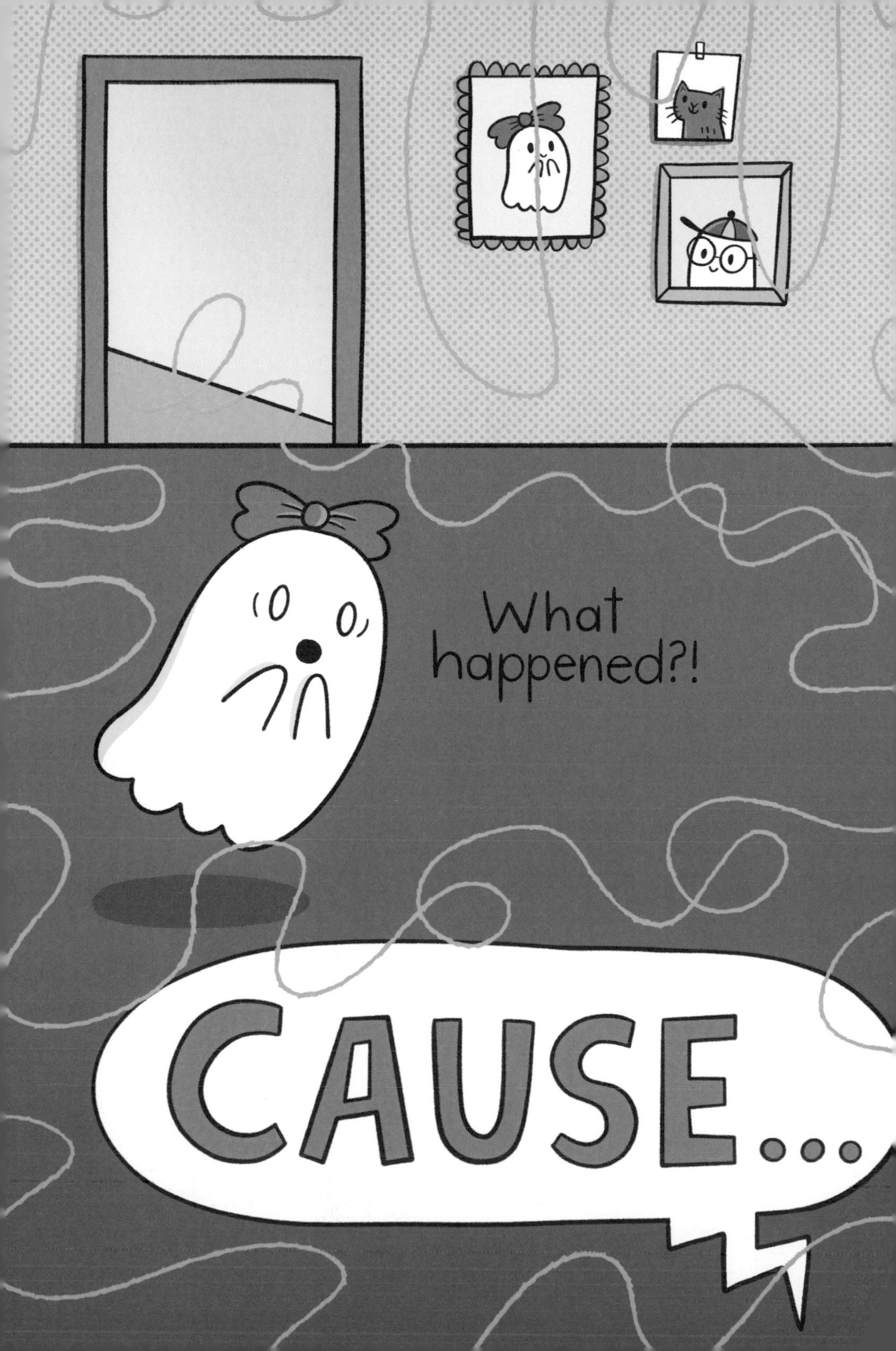
What happened?!
CAUSE...

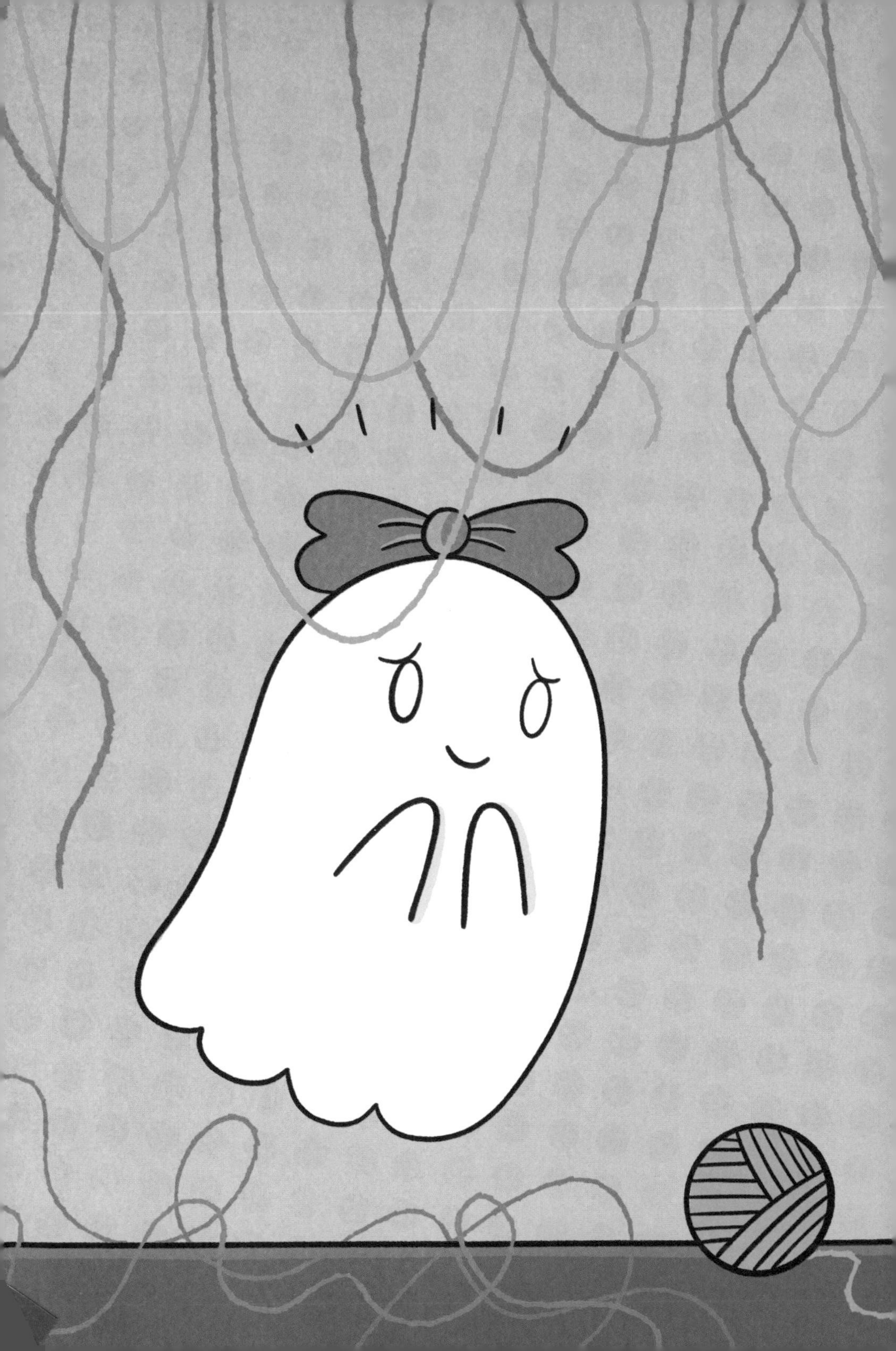

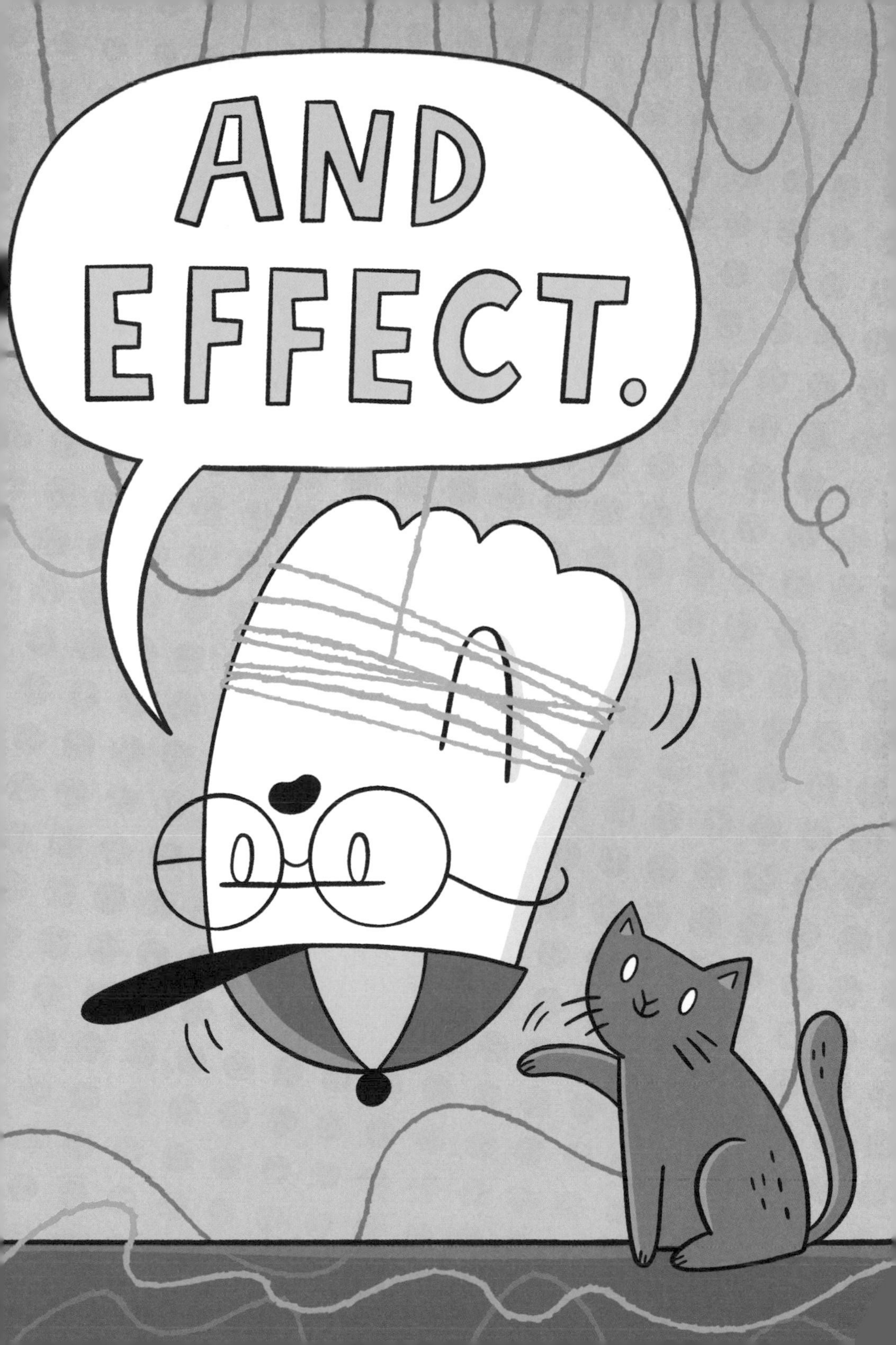
AND EFFECT.

Triple Play

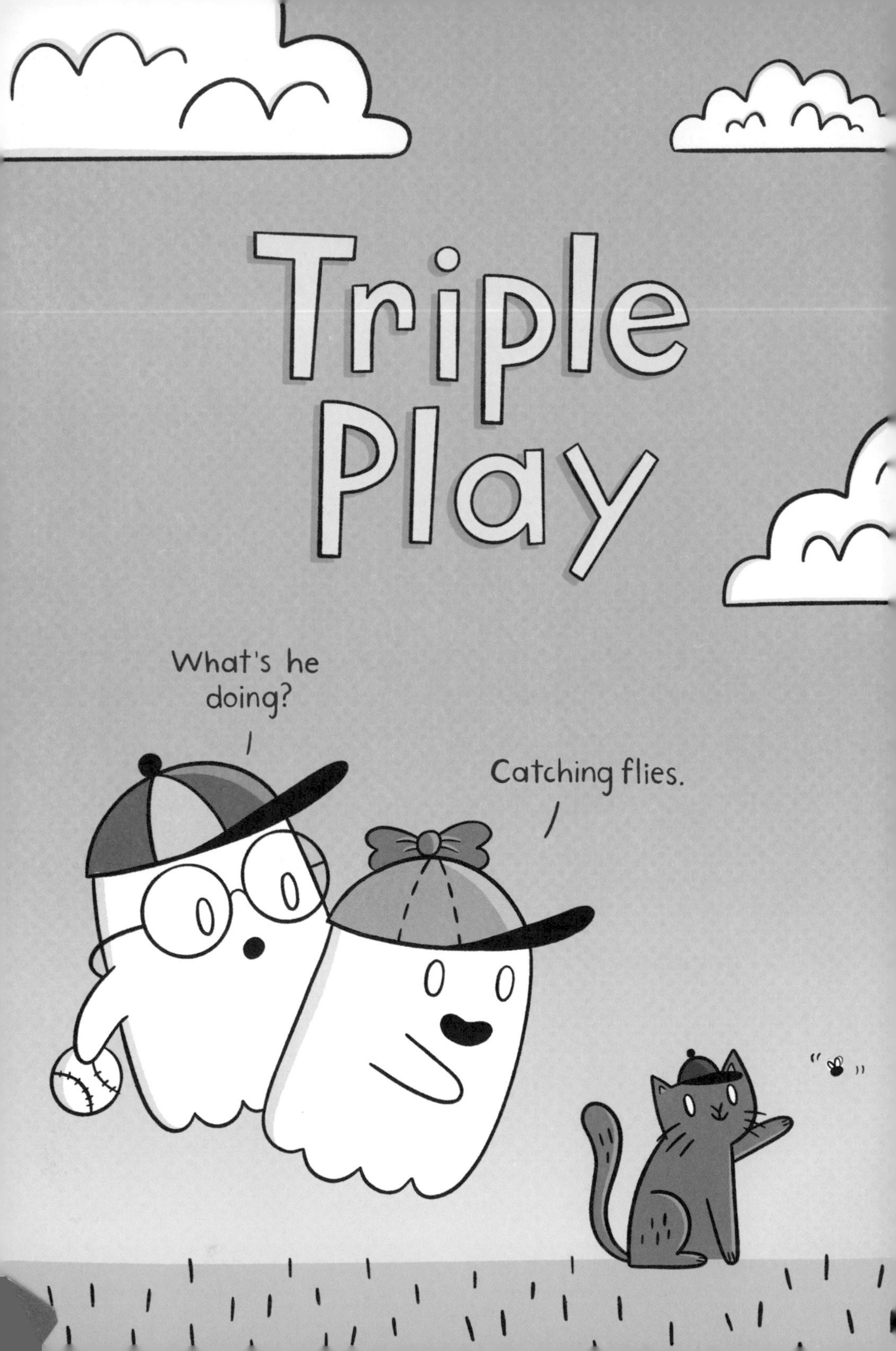
What's he doing?
Catching flies.

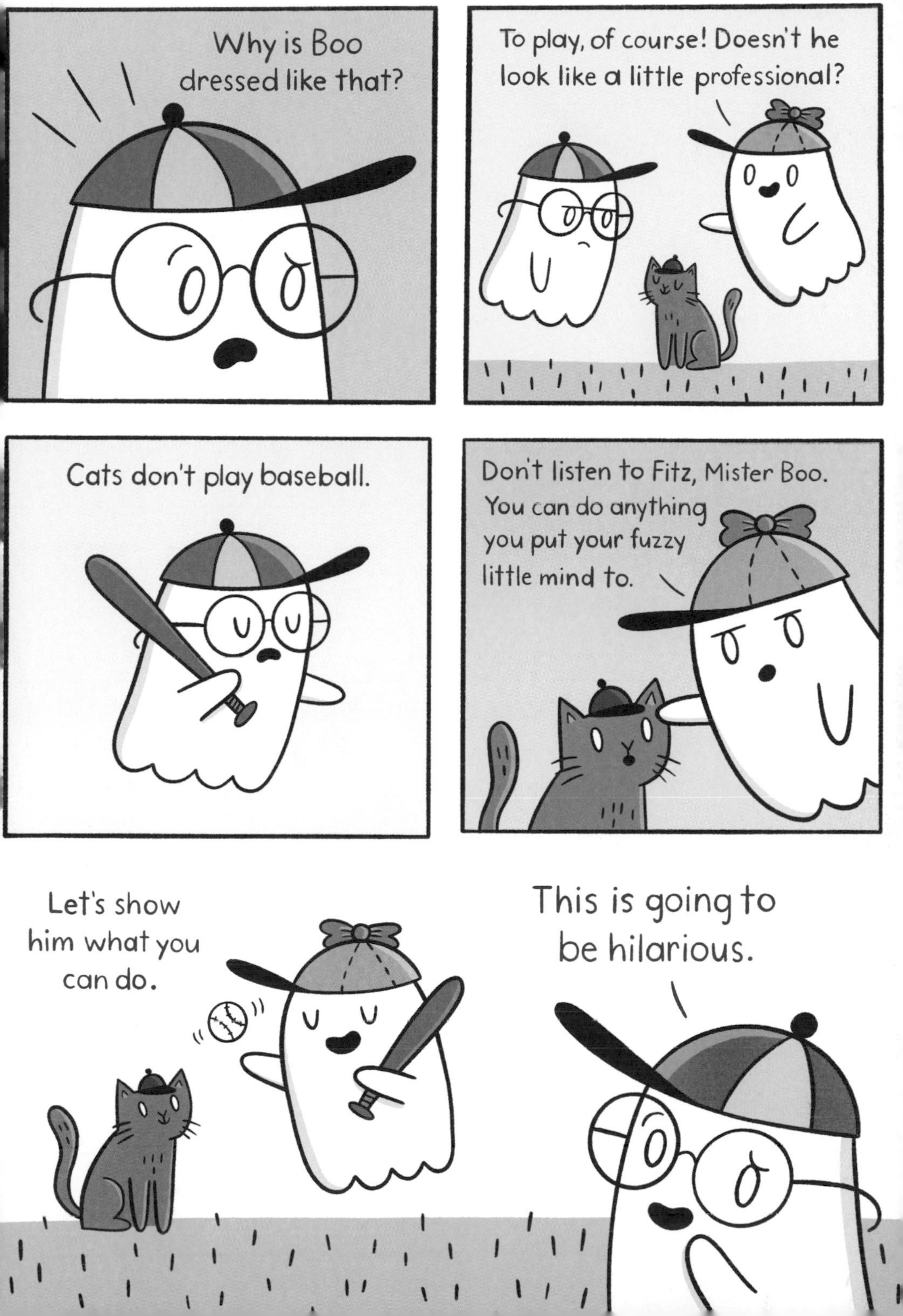
Why is Boo dressed like that?
To play, of course! Doesn't he look like a little professional?
Cats don't play baseball.
Don't listen to Fitz, Mister Boo. You can do anything you put your fuzzy little mind to.
Let's show him what you can do.
This is going to be hilarious.

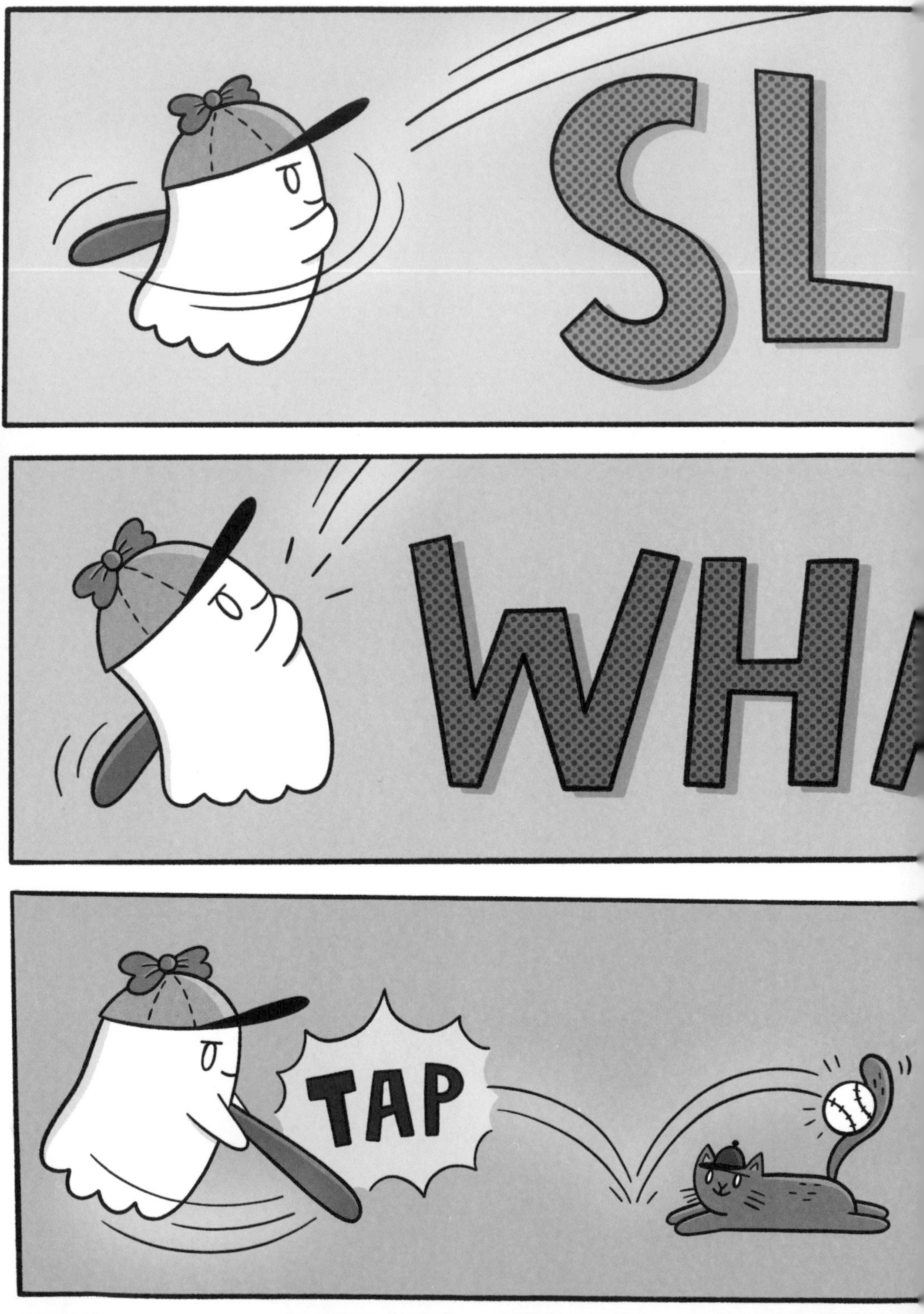
SL
WH
TAP

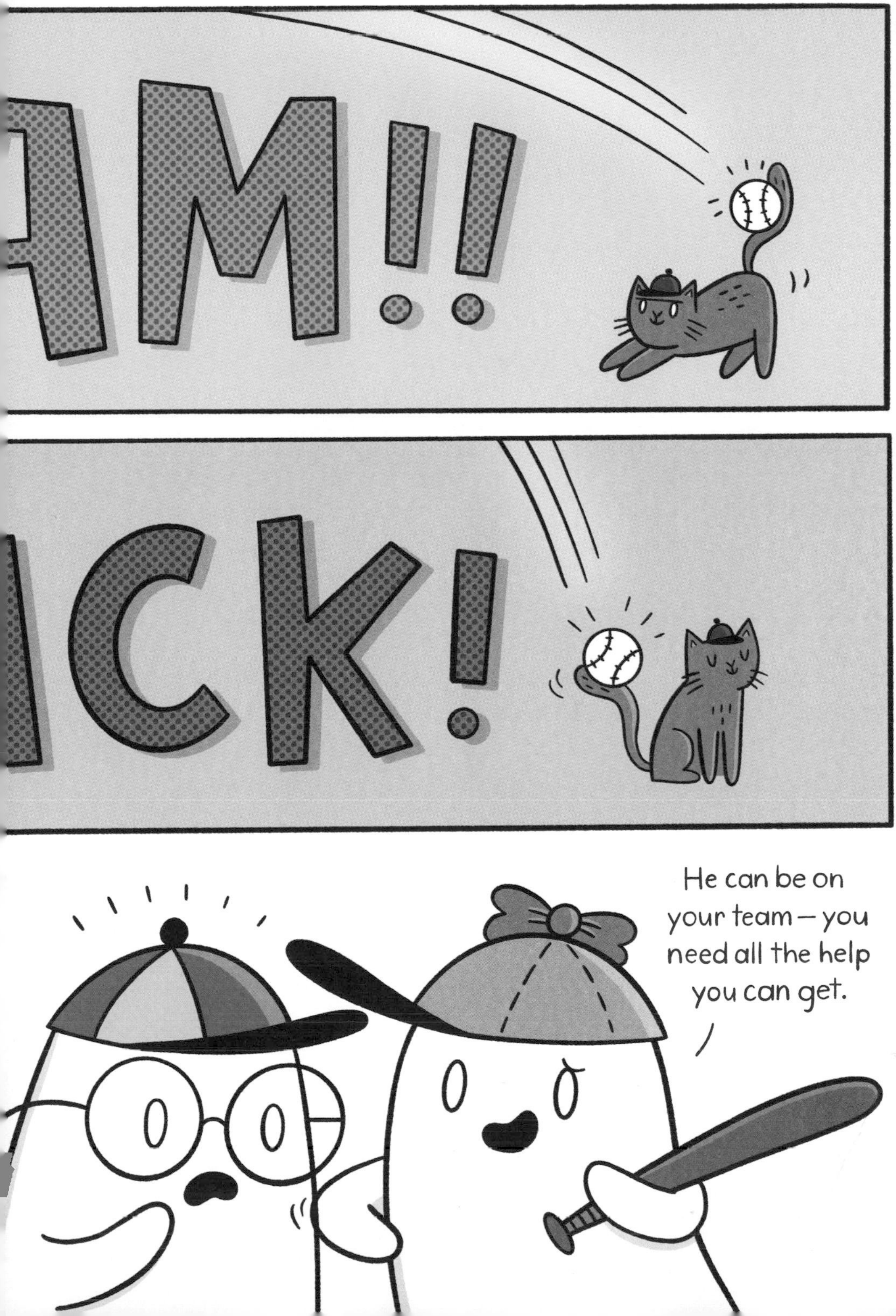
AM!!
ICK!
He can be on your team—you need all the help you can get.

For Science

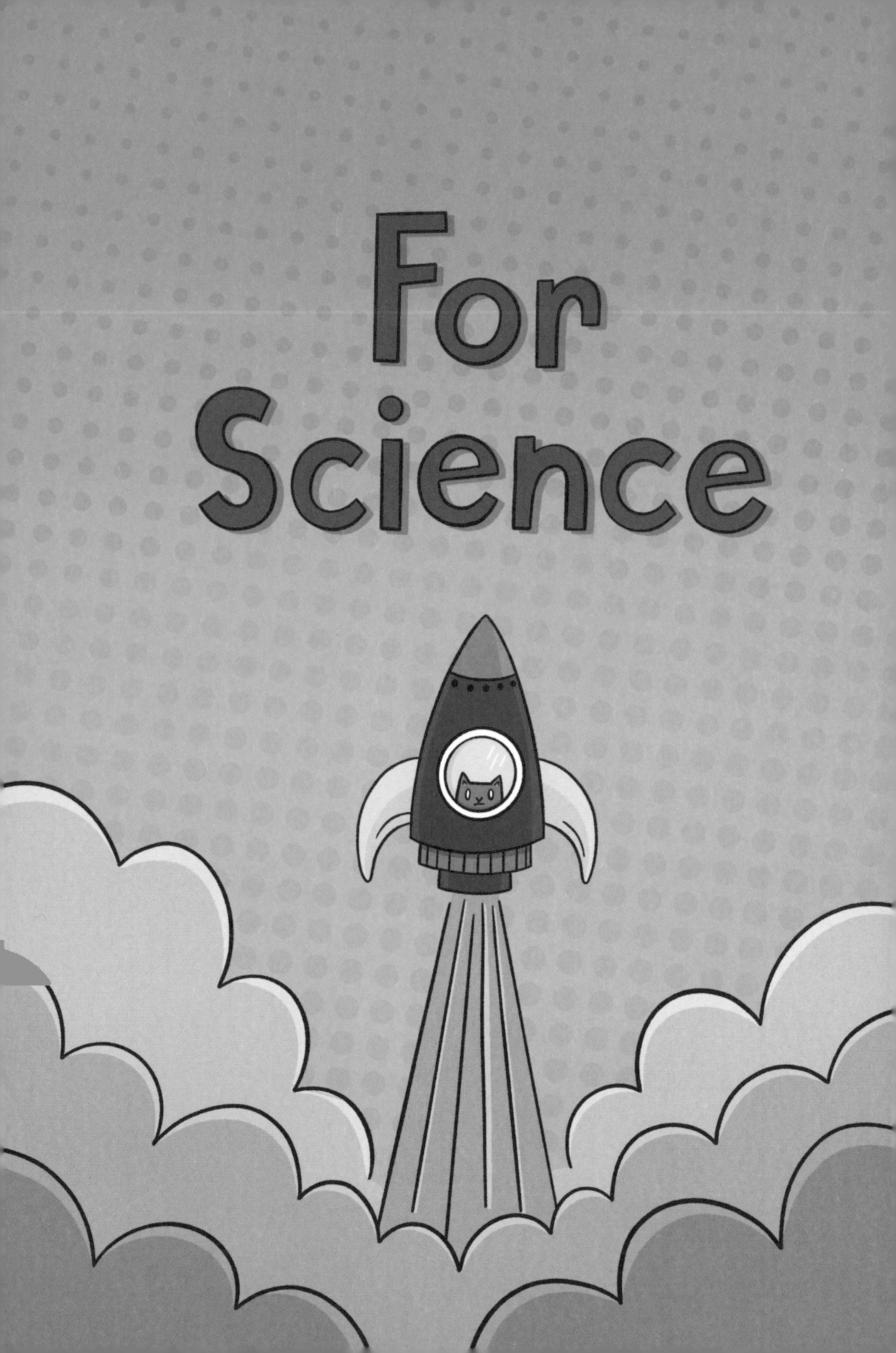

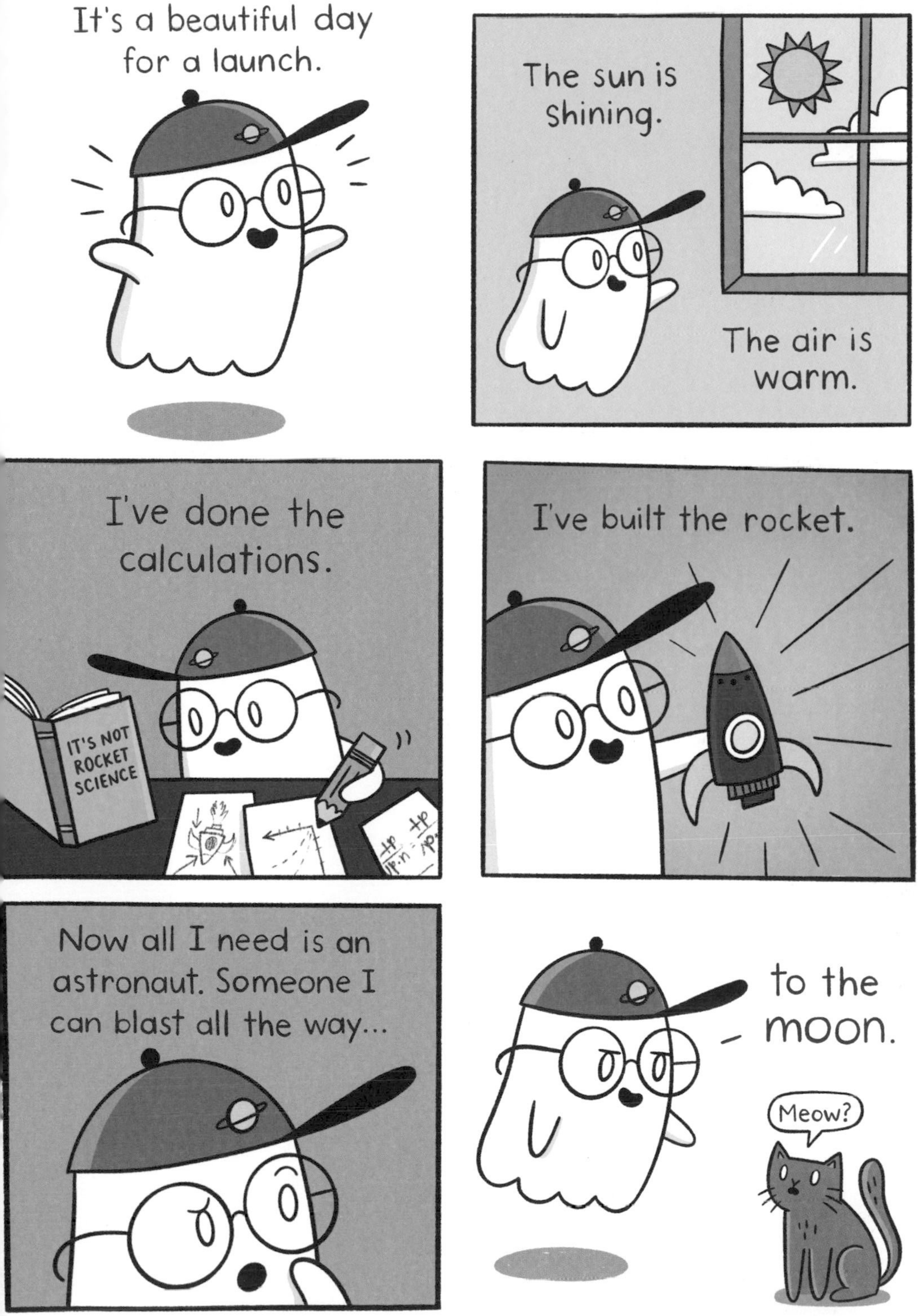
It's a beautiful day for a launch.
The sun is shining.
The air is warm.
I've done the calculations.
IT'S NOT ROCKET SCIENCE
I've built the rocket.
Now all I need is an astronaut. Someone I can blast all the way...
– to the moon.
Meow?

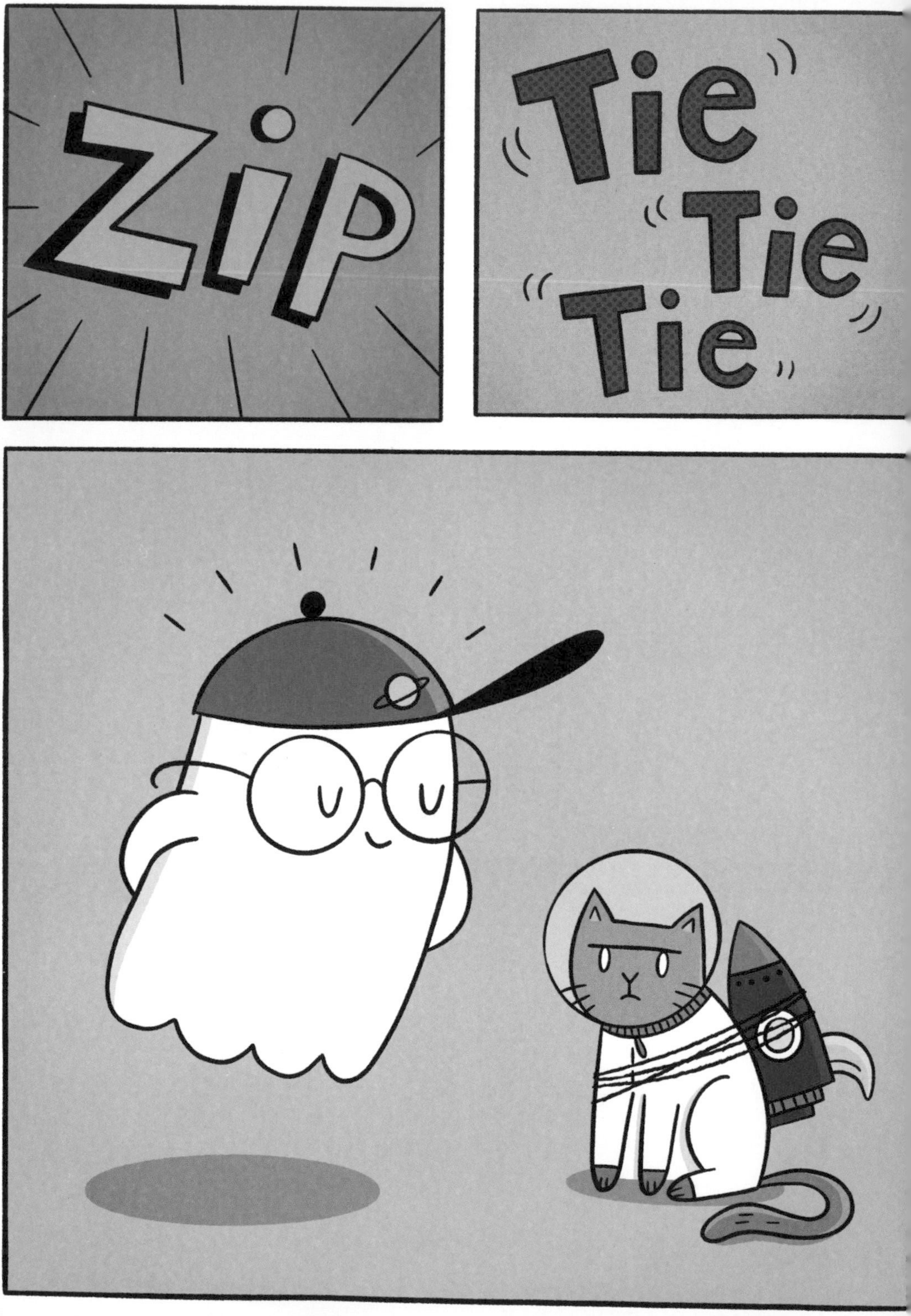
ZIP
Tie
Tie
Tie

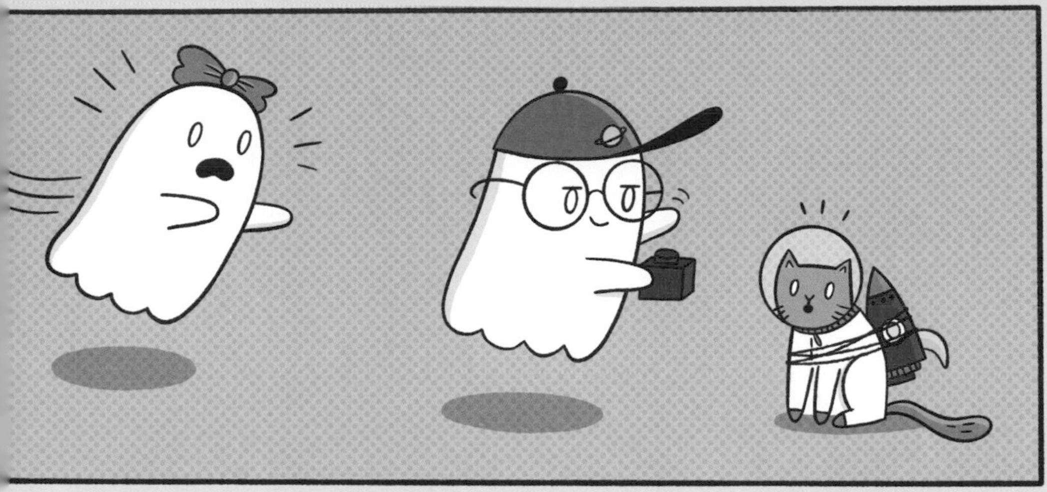

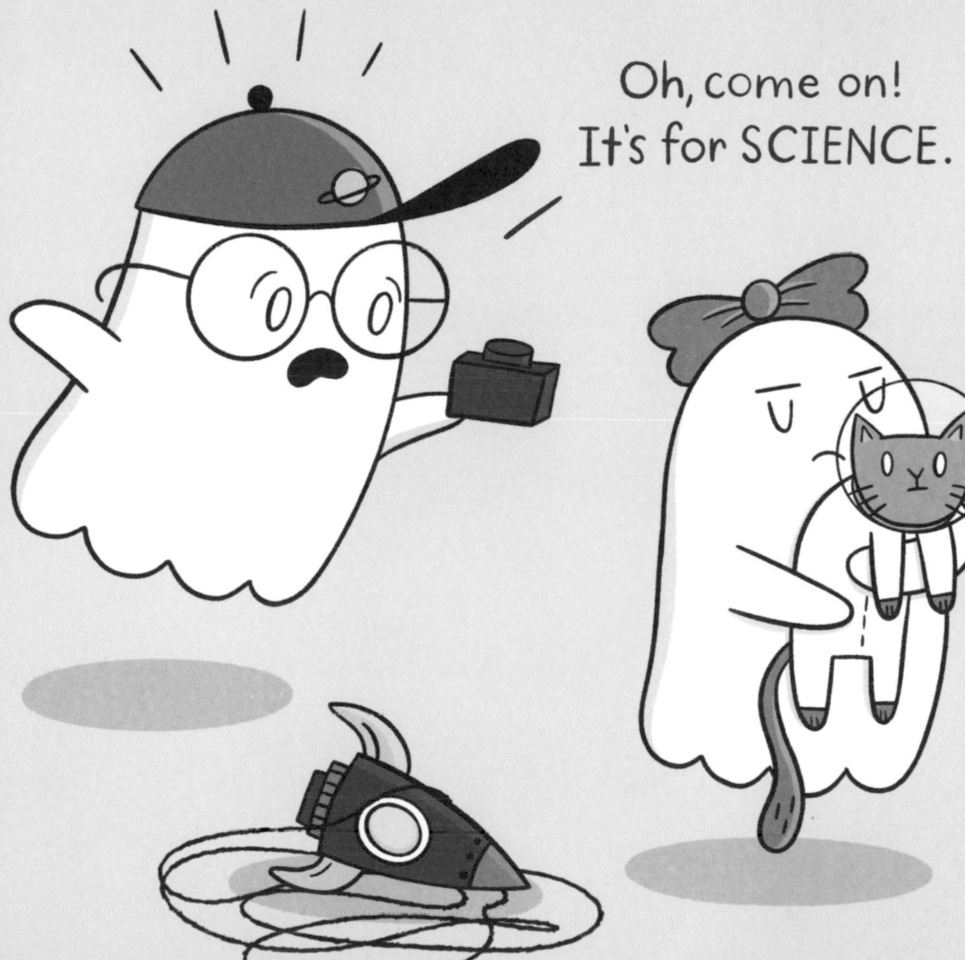
Oh, come on!
It's for SCIENCE.

Stargazing

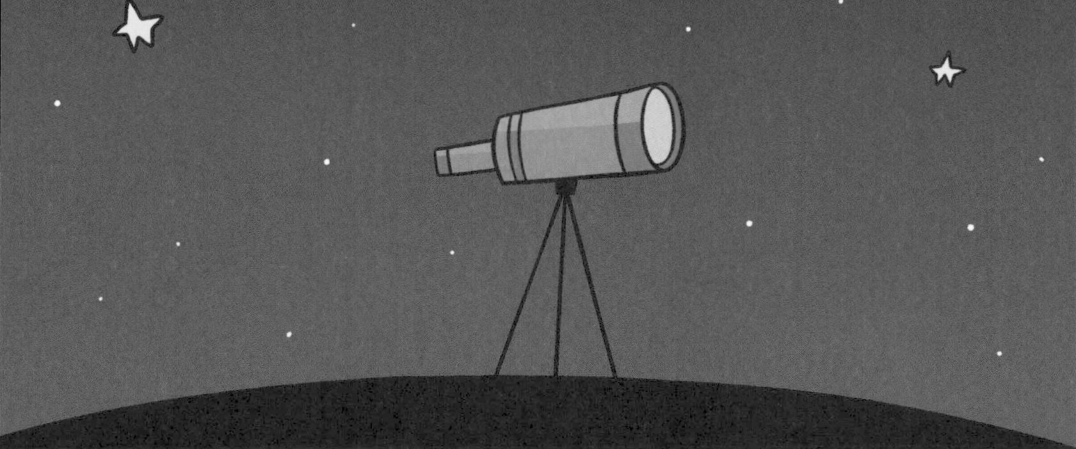

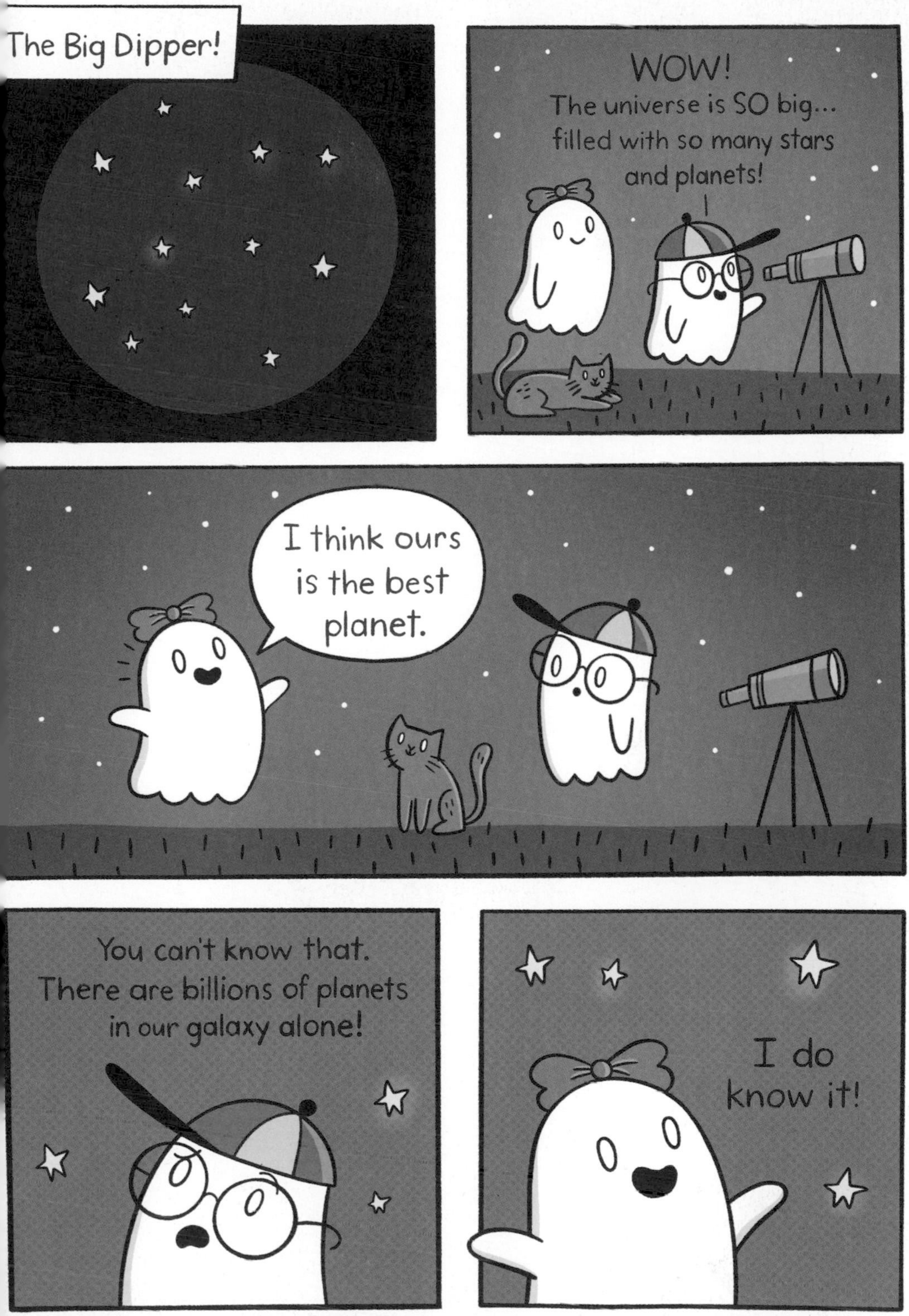
The Big Dipper!
WOW!
The universe is SO big... filled with so many stars and planets!
I think ours is the best planet.
You can't know that. There are billions of planets in our galaxy alone!
I do know it!

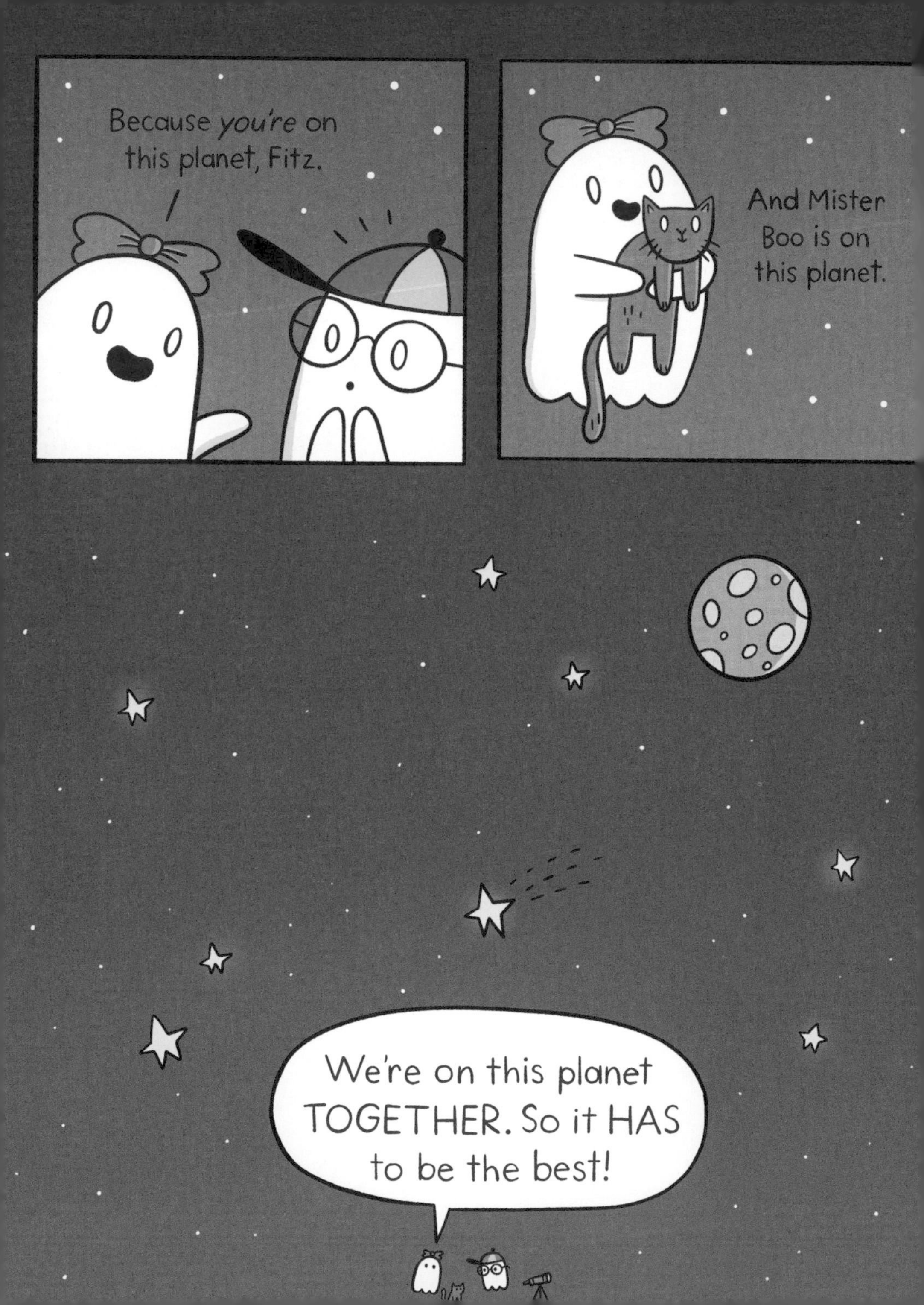
Because *you're* on this planet, Fitz.
And Mister Boo is on this planet.
We're on this planet TOGETHER. So it HAS to be the best!

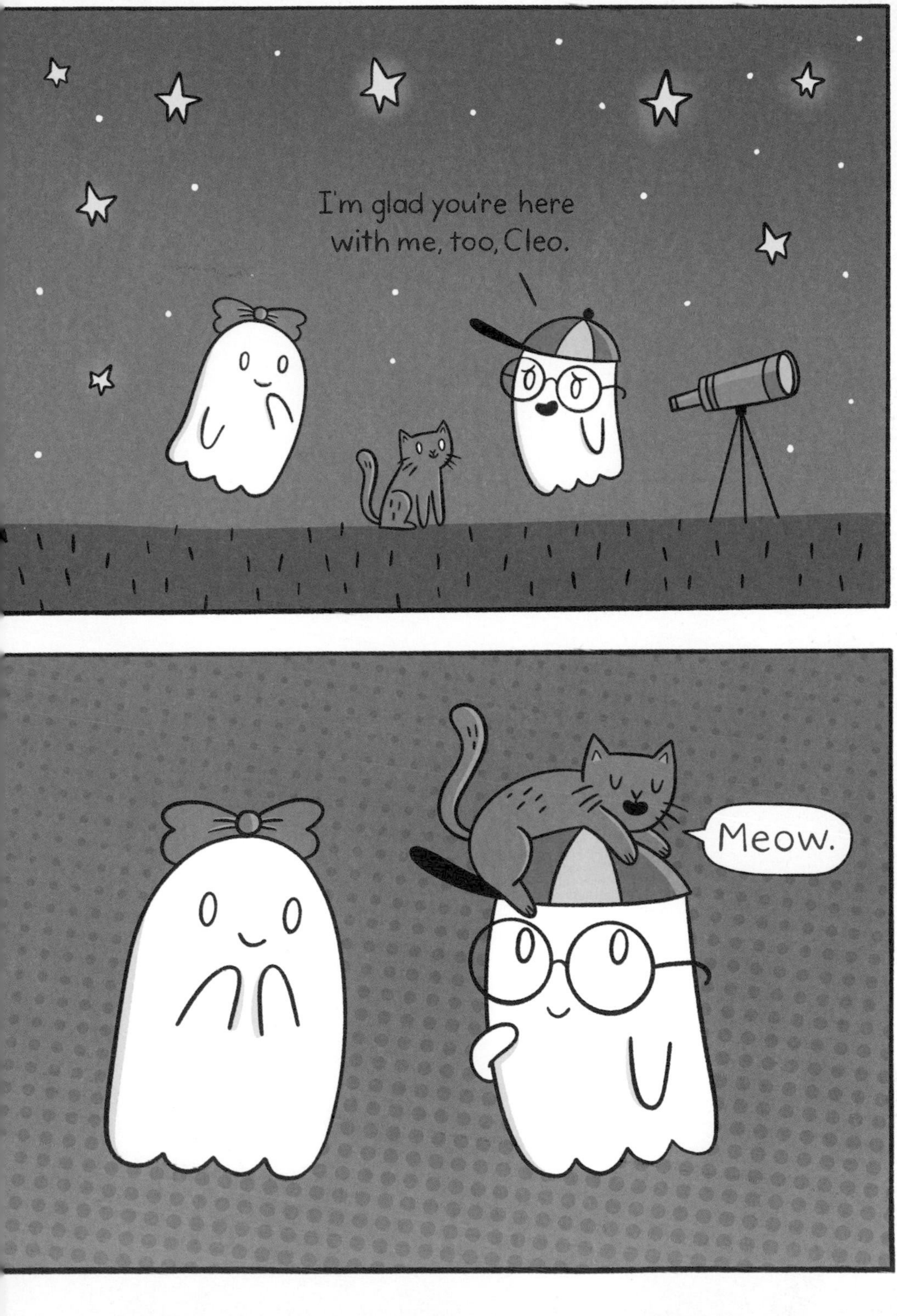
I'm glad you're here with me, too, Cleo.
Meow.

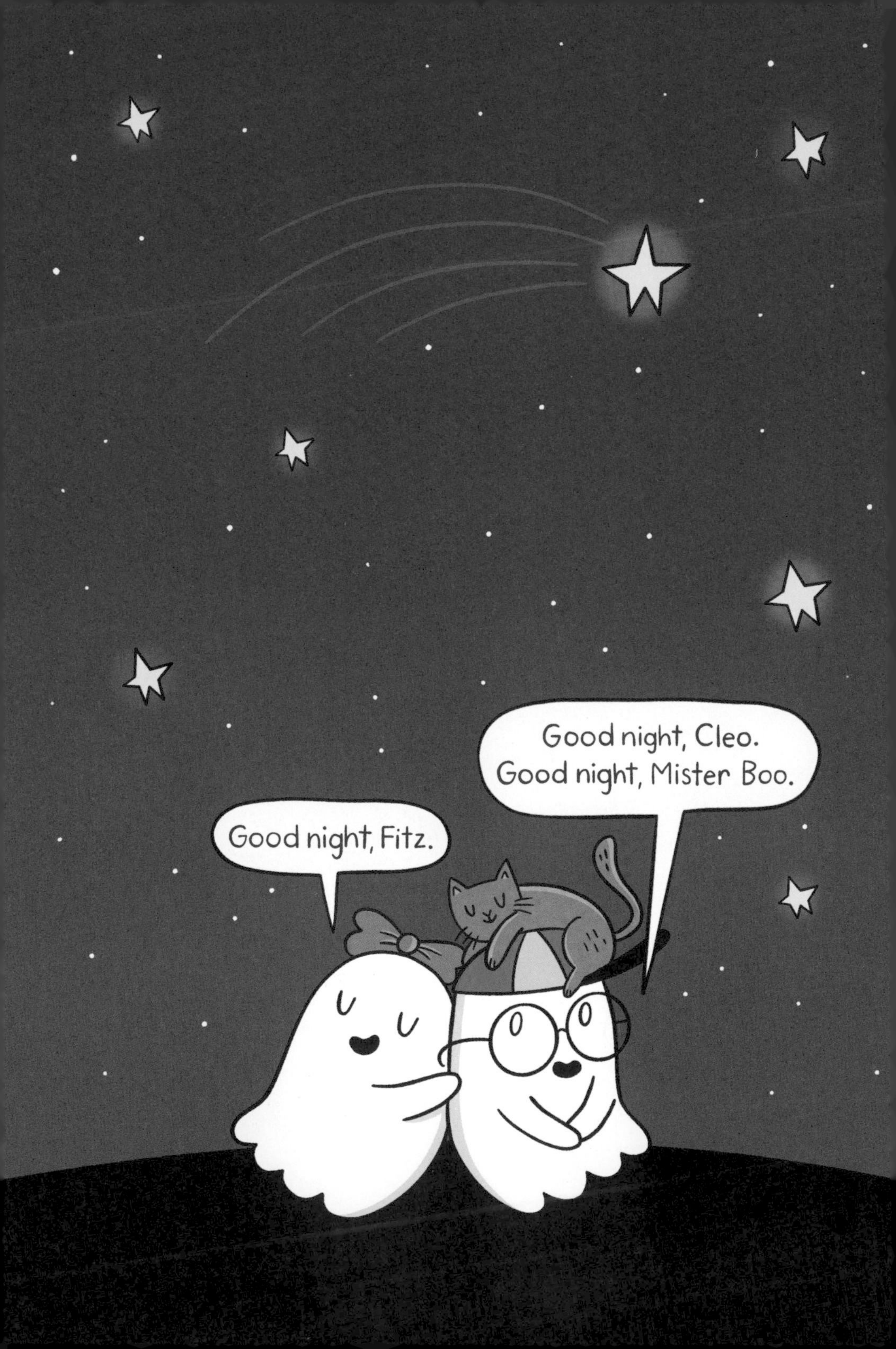
Good night, Cleo.
Good night, Mister Boo.
Good night, Fitz.

An exclusive first glimpse of the next book
in the Fitz and Cleo series:

Fitz
AND
Cleo

Get Creative

Head
in the
Clouds

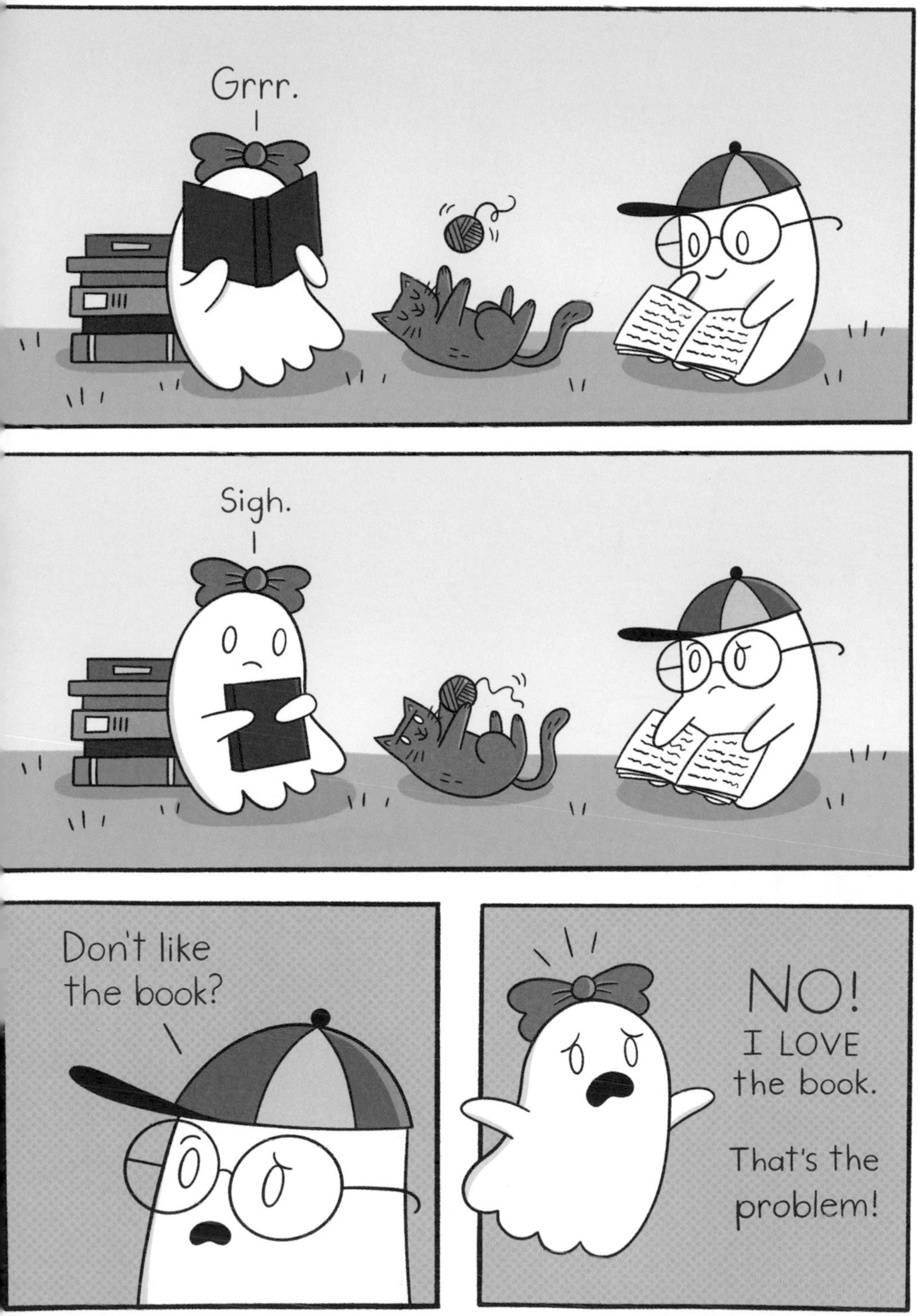
Grrr.
Sigh.
Don't like the book?
NO!
I LOVE the book.
That's the problem!

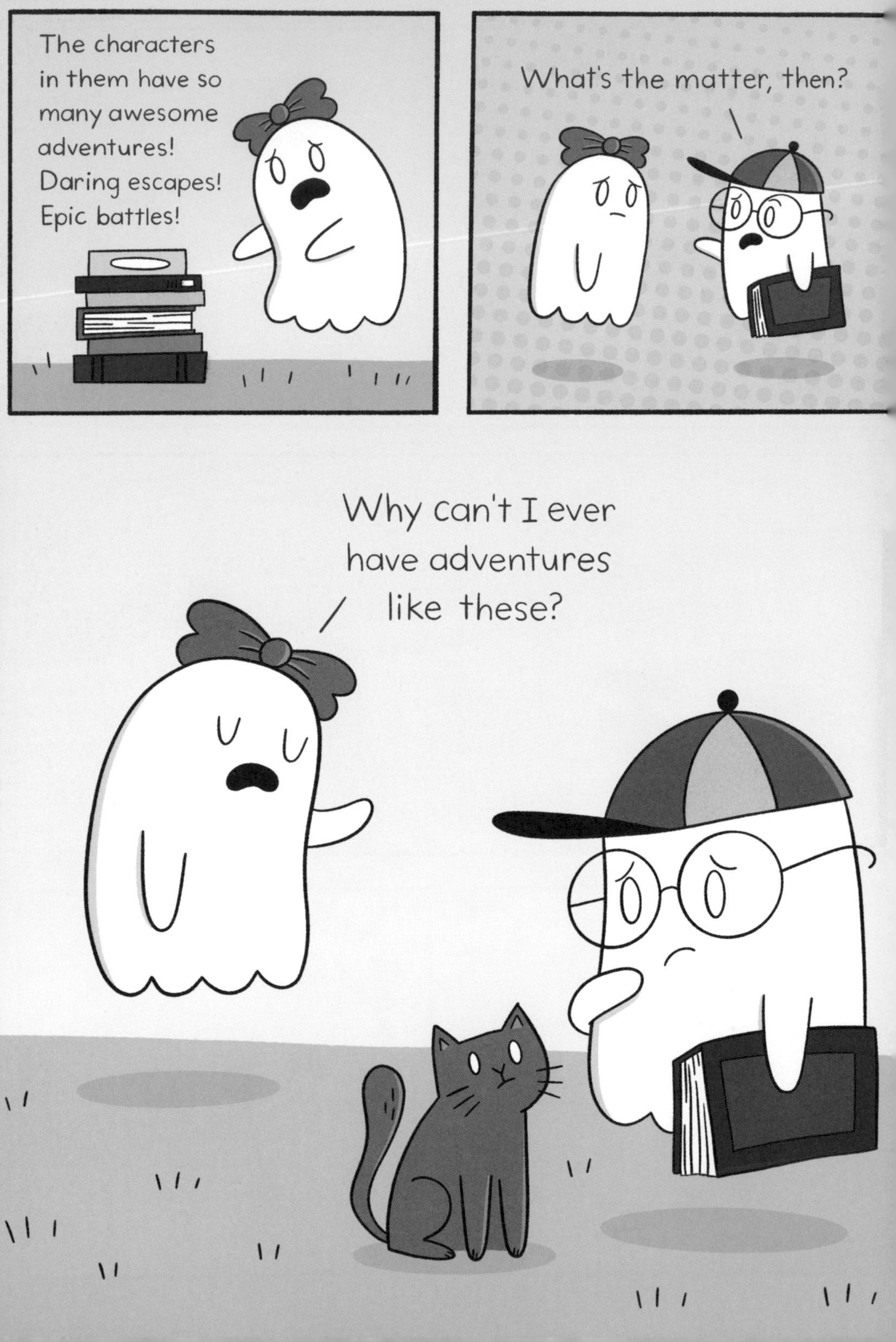
The characters in them have so many awesome adventures! Daring escapes! Epic battles!
What's the matter, then?
Why can't I ever have adventures like these?

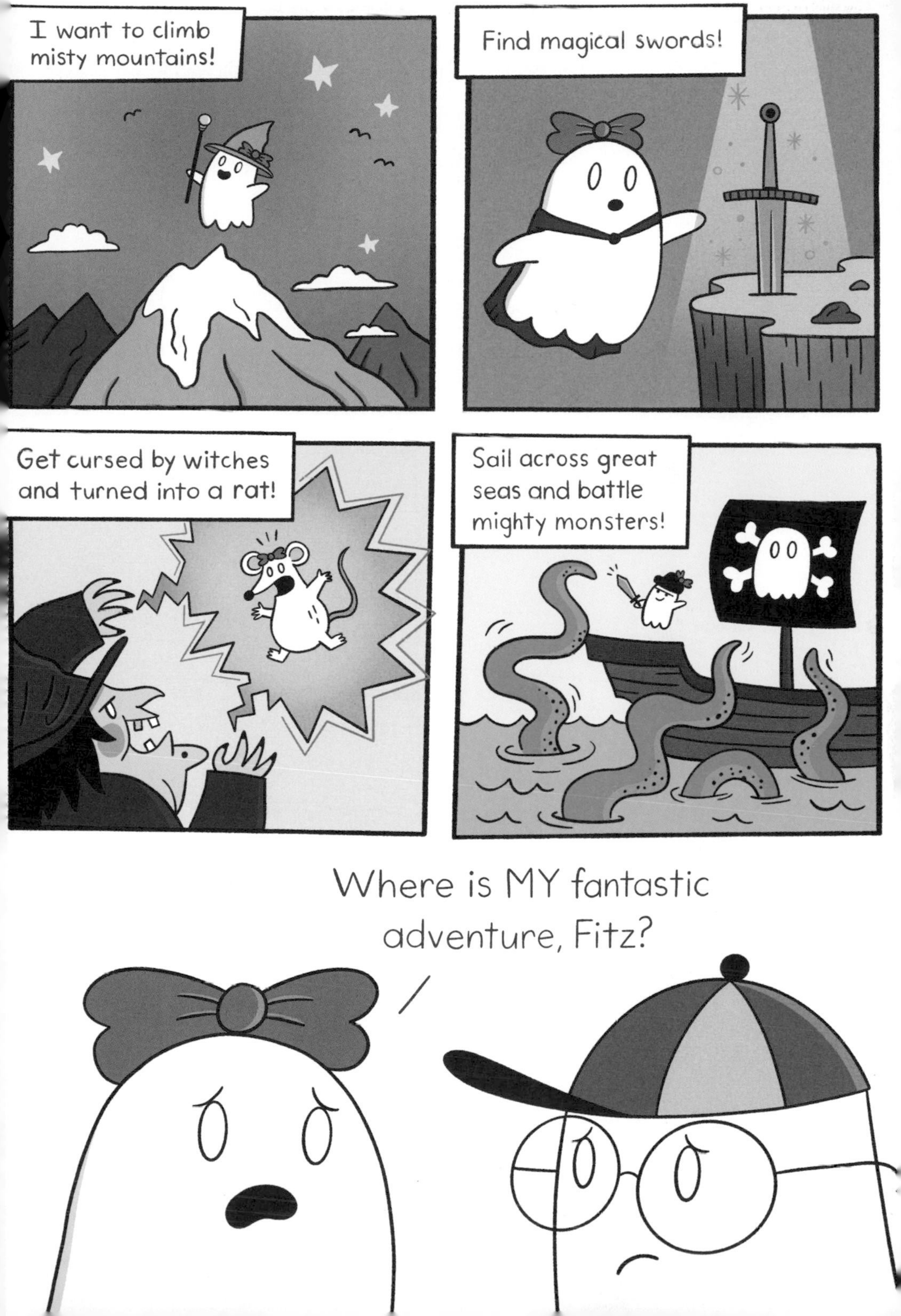
I want to climb misty mountains!
Find magical swords!
Get cursed by witches and turned into a rat!
Sail across great seas and battle mighty monsters!
Where is MY fantastic adventure, Fitz?

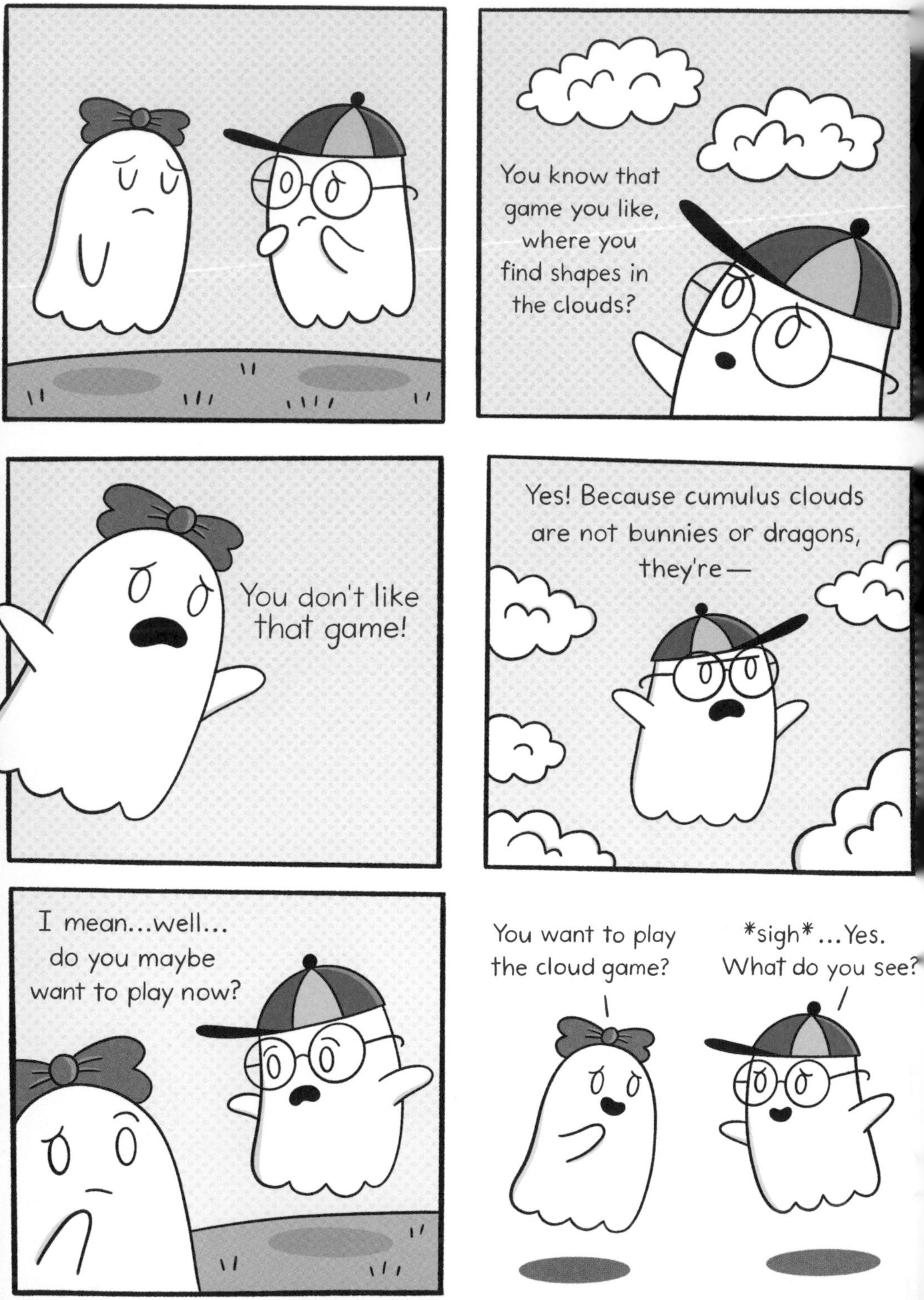

You know that game you like, where you find shapes in the clouds?
You don't like that game!
Yes! Because cumulus clouds are not bunnies or dragons, they're—
I mean...well... do you maybe want to play now?
You want to play the cloud game?
sigh...Yes. What do you see?

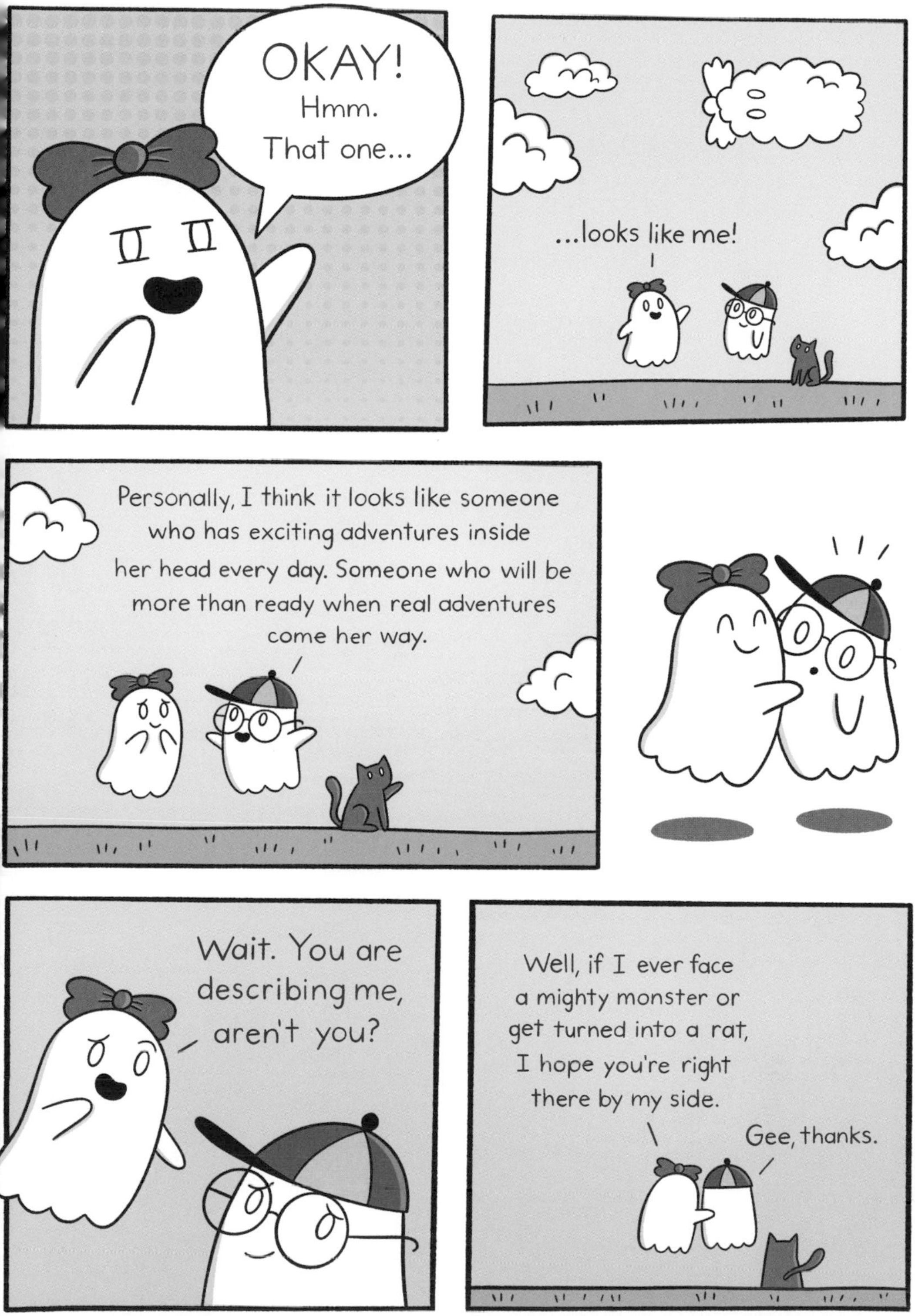
OKAY! Hmm. That one...
...looks like me!
Personally, I think it looks like someone who has exciting adventures inside her head every day. Someone who will be more than ready when real adventures come her way.
Wait. You are describing me, aren't you?
Well, if I ever face a mighty monster or get turned into a rat, I hope you're right there by my side.
Gee, thanks.

Happy-go-lucky Cleo and science buff Fitz are BACK and they are feeling . . . inspired (much to their cat, Mister Boo's, dismay).

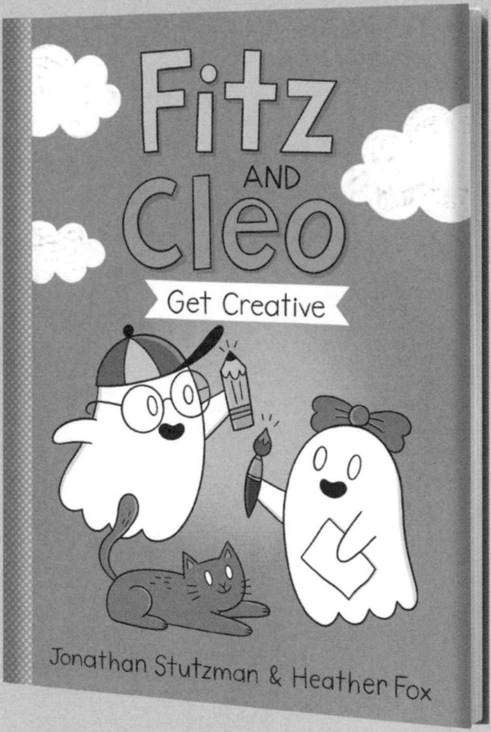
Fitz
AND
Cleo
Get Creative
Jonathan Stutzman & Heather Fox

Join the most adorable siblings this way of the afterlife through ten gut-busting creative farces, including flexing their storytelling muscles with ghost stories and writing, casting, and producing their first film.

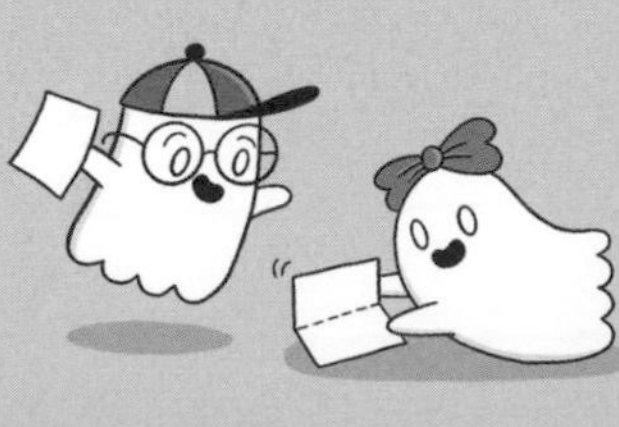

For Lauren, my Fitz – H.F.
To my Buddy – J.S.

An imprint of Macmillan Publishing Group, LLC
120 Broadway, New York, NY 10271 • mackids.com

Text copyright © 2021 by Jonathan Stutzman.
Illustrations copyright © 2021 by Heather Fox.
All rights reserved.

Square Fish and the Square Fish logo are trademarks of Macmillan and are
used by Henry Holt and Company under license from Macmillan.
Our books may be purchased in bulk for promotional, educational, or
business use. Please contact your local bookseller or the Macmillan
Corporate and Premium Sales Department at (800) 221-7945 ext. 5442 or
by email at MacmillanSpecialMarkets@macmillan.com.

Library of Congress Cataloging-in-Publication Data is available.

Originally published in the United States by Henry Holt and Company
First Square Fish edition, 2022

Book designed by Mike Burroughs

Square Fish logo designed by Filomena Tuosto

Printed in China by Toppan Leefung Printing Ltd.,
Dongguan City, Guangdong Province.

ISBN 978-1-250-83264-1 (paperback)